CORAZÓN

CORAZÓN

A Collecton of Short Stories

SAMUEL PROVENZANO

CORAZON CREATES
Oregon House, CA

Dedication

It has been an honor to teach and to learn from the many students who have come through my writing classes. Thank you, and I dedicate this book to you.

Contents

Introduction

The stories in this book have resulted from seeing the world mainly from the heart. The way we see the world relies mostly on what we've experienced and how we've processed and transformed those experiences into a perspective. If we become our own person and rely on what we see and hear and live, removed from all the incoming noises that try to convince us how we should see, we can become closer to an honest story of our own.

Corazón

heart, soulful, where love resides with persistence

1

Al

He was an old guy, standing on the boardwalk, a cane and a brown paper bag in one hand and a fishing rod in the other.

"Catch anything?" I asked.

"Naw, nothing much to catch here," he said. He looked sad.

"My boat is in that slip over there," I said; "you want to come out with me?

"Sure," he said. "My name is Al," he called to me as he walked along behind me. I stopped and shook his hand.

"Sam," I said.

He stood about six feet tall, was dark complexioned and had a goatee.

I stepped into the boat and offered him my hand as he boarded. We rode out to my favorite spot on the lake, baited our lines and casted out. We didn't say much for a while.

"Got kids?" he asked.

"No," I said. "You?"

"Yeah," he said. "My daughter brought me out here; she's worried about me. I had heart surgery, and she wants me to live with her. She's out looking for a place for us right now." After a moment he added, "Got two sons too. One of them is two hundred and eighty-nine pounds, and the other has a heart of gold. I'd like you to meet him some time."

"Yeah, I'd like to," I said.

"You married?" He asked.

"Yes," I said, "for twenty-four years now. Your wife pass?"

No," he said. "I came home from work one day after thirty-five years with her, and she said she didn't want to live with me anymore."

"Wow, that's pretty tough," I said.

"I'm better off," he said. We were quiet for a while.

"Can I have one of your cold drinks?" he asked. I looked at the bag he was pointing to by his feet and then I remembered he had the bag in his hand that held the cane as he boarded the boat.

"Uh, sure, but those are yours."

"Oh yeah, that's right," he said and smiled. "Sometimes I forget things," he said.

"Me too," I said.

After a while, he said, "You have kids?"

"Nope," I said.

"I have three," he said. "Two sons and a daughter." Remembering that he had just told me that information, I looked at him to see if he was joking.

We talked about the coming election and the problems the future generations would face because of greed, and we talked about music and how much we both preferred Stevie Wonder to rap.

"Can I have one of your sandwiches? He asked, pointing to the bag at his feet.

"That's yours, Al," I said.

"Aw, that's right; you want half?" he asked. I shook my head.

We fished for a couple of hours, and I was ready to head back.

"Shall we try another time?" I asked.

"Sure, tomorrow's good for me, but you're the captain, he said.

As we approached the boat dock, I saw a flurry of activity. A security officer and a small crowd of people were milling around the dock, and I wondered what was wrong. As I tied my boat in my slip, the security officer came to my boat.

"Man, we were worried about you, Al. Your family has been frantic; nobody knew where you were."

Al stepped out of the boat and waited for me.

"Thanks man," he said. "If ever you need my help with anything, you let me know."

"Thank you Al; I enjoyed it too."

The security guard came to my boat again after Al left.

"His family was really worried about him," he said. "He has dementia, and they didn't know what to think. I'm sure glad he was with you."

The next day, I showed up at the dock to keep

my promise about taking Al out, but he wasn't there. I walked over to the front office and asked the girl at the desk which site he was at, and she told me that they had left the previous evening.

Then she handed me a package with an envelope attached to it. I read the note that was in the envelope:

Dear Sam,

Thanks for a day I won't soon forget. You can never guess how important your kindness to this stranger has been. Please accept this gift. I'll never use it again, and though it's only a token of how much I appreciate your friendship, I'm comforted to know you'll value it more than anyone else I can think of.

Your Friend,

Al

I opened the package slowly, wishing I could have told him that I enjoyed his company too, and inside the box there was one of the most beautiful fishing rods I'd ever seen. It was in two parts, and it was made of hickory. In the same box was a very unusual and vintage reel of the finest quality. There was also an assortment of very rare and expensive lures and miscellaneous fishing gear.

Months later I received a phone call from Al's

daughter informing me that Al had passed in his sleep the night before. He had inquired at the front desk of the marina what my contact information was weeks prior to his passing. She said he had spoken often of our brief encounter that morning and that she would be forever grateful for the joy I had brought to her dad through that one kindness.

Now, as I reflect on that one morning and that one encounter, I realize that we never know how these moments that we sometimes view as so ordinary can impact forever the people we meet. It was Al's gratitude for what was for me a simple shared experience of something we both enjoyed, that helped me see how much there is to be grateful for.

2

Corazón

Francisco:

My name is Francisco Esparta, and I've been playing accordion for thirty-three years. I play mostly music from my homeland, which is Spain, but I love gypsy music from all cultures, so I sometimes play my favorite gypsy melodies from memory. I've played for parties, weddings, and at restaurants, but lately I've been playing in the streets of New York for anyone who likes my playing. People often leave me tips and make requests of music they wish to hear. Many of the requests are American tunes which I've never heard. They leave me tips anyway.

Lately a dog has begun to follow me home after I've been playing. He is a medium-sized dog, and he is gold with black whiskers. I live on the second floor of a building; it is an apartment above a grocery store. When I look out my window, down at the street below after I've been playing all day, the dog is gone. But he shows up to where I play each day, and he sits by my side quietly when I play. He seems to enjoy the sound of the accordion and the music it makes. Though I don't play in the same place each day, the dog continues to find me, and he waits patiently until I'm finished for the day.

Corazón:

My dear friend who has passed away called me Corazón. He gave me food and shelter for all the years we were together. He played music on a box-shaped thing like this stranger plays. It brings me peace to hear this music again. Sometimes I cry at night because I miss my friend so much. This stranger seems to know and play the same songs my friend used to play. It brings me back happiness to hear these sounds again. I wish I could tell the stranger how grateful I am for reminding me that we have much to live for.

The other day, when this new stranger finished for the day, as he packed up, he reached out his hand to me and when I drew close, he patted my head. No one has patted my head in such a long time and, though I was afraid and I felt a growl in my throat, I let him pet me. He gave me a piece of cheese and a hunk of bread. I watched the stranger's eyes, and it seemed to me he was very kind. He spoke to me gently and though I didn't understand the words, I'm sure he intended to be my friend. I thanked him with a lick on his hand. After he wiped his hand on his pants, he patted my head again.

Francisco:

Today, as I played in a new location, there was a larger group of people than usual who stopped to hear me play. One man set his hat upside down on the ground before me, and people began to fill the hat with not only coins but paper bills as well. The dog watched as people stepped forward and placed the money in the hat. He seemed to understand because he wagged his tail each time some one new gave money. Many of the people seemed happy; the sun was shining. One young couple began to dance, and then another, and before long, there were many couples dancing to my music.

The dog became very excited as he watched the people dance and at one point, he began to make a high-pitched sound in his throat. It did not sound like an angry sound or a bark, but like an attempt to sing with my music. What made it so special was that he seemed to be listening closely enough to be in tune with the music. When I looked at him, I swear he was smiling. As I listened to his sounds, I found myself humming audibly with him. After the tune was over, a young woman stepped out of the crowd and placed a bowl of water before him. He went to it and drank the entire bowl.

Corazón:

My new friend played even more beautifully today, and people were dancing. I found myself singing along with his melodies, and he began singing too. When I followed my friend home tonight, after his performance, he invited me into his home. I was reluctant at first, but he insisted and once inside, he gave me a bowl of water and a bowl of food, which was delicious. I didn't realize how hungry I was. After I ate and drank my fill, he sat on the floor next to me and patted me. He spoke softly to me until I fell asleep. I slept better than I had slept in a long time. It was a relief to be off the streets and safe.

When I awoke the next morning, my new friend let me out and, soon after, he came outside with his music box, and I followed him to a busy street corner where he played for people passing by. Many people, who seemed to be in such hurry one moment, stopped abruptly when they heard him play. The faces of those who listened changed dramatically after a few moments. People seemed less frantic and more at peace, and the transformation was almost immediate. One of the passers by, a beautiful young woman with fire-red hair and laughing dark eyes, came to me and gave me a delicious bone, and she said my name.

Francisco:

Last night, I brought the dog inside. He was very well-mannered and, though he seemed a little uncertain at first, he soon made himself at home. I'm not sure how long he has lived in the streets, but he seems very grateful for every small kindness. I'm finding that his companionship has given new meaning to my life. When I look into his eyes, I see an ever growing trust as well as something I'm a little afraid to name. It's as though he reads my thoughts. He requires nothing of me, but he is constantly focused on me.

Last evening, as we were finishing up for the day, an attractive red-haired woman brought a huge bone to the dog. As he gently took it from her, she came to me.

"You have a beautiful dog", she said. "What's his name?"

Her question stopped me; it had never occurred to me to name the dog or that he was "my" dog. In fact, I thought of him as my equal, and neither of us belonged to each other. We were friends who had found each other.

"He's a stray," I said. "I haven't named him yet. What do you think I should name him?" Her eyes sparkled as she thought for a moment.

"Well," she said, "his eyes are very emotional, so he has a lot of heart and you look and sound Spanish. How about something Spanish and passionate, Corazón?

The dog's ears immediately stood upright.

"Ah, yes," I said. "Corazón is the perfect name for him. He seems to like it as well."

Corazón:

The woman with the red hair came to my friend's home tonight carrying a bag. She prepared dinner for my friend, and they shared their food with me. I heard my friend call the woman Rose. I still wonder how she knew my name. Rose called my friend Francisco. After we all ate, they asked me to sit and then they asked me to shake hands with them. They laughed as I obeyed each of their commands. At one point, I had to relieve myself, so I scratched at the door. They praised me and patted me and then they let me out. When I finished, I scratched at the door, and they let me in.

I sat in a corner as they drank red liquid from long stem glasses. Francisco took out his music box and began to play, and Rose removed a black box from her purse and assembled a long tubular musical instrument; she began to play music with Francisco, and it was so lovely, I began to sing. When we were done, Francisco said we were the Corazón trio. I thought then, and I believe now that humans could be so much more of what they are if they could just stop trying to be so many things that they're not. My heart was full. I found myself lying with my head between my front paws.

3

Hookey

_____

Mario Favone noticed how, when the teacher called on the pretty black girl named Yolanda Coleman, the girl was always poised. She had a soft calm voice and a way of speaking, walking, standing, that caused Mario to dream of her.

He'd only spoken to her twice, once when she came to his table at the school cafeteria and asked if he was through with the saltshaker, and once when they both arrived at the pencil sharpener at the same time and he insisted that she go first.

Now he stood on the front steps of P.S. 114 and

watched as the police handcuffed Yolanda's hands behind her back. He saw her face as they put her in the back seat of the squad car, and he felt a stinging sensation behind his eyes, his legs felt shaky, and his breathing was irregular.

Yolanda was thirteen years old, and Mario was sure that she was the most beautiful girl in school. Her black skin had a light of its own, and her eyes always seemed to be searching for the hidden meaning of things. She wore her hair in dreadlocks, and the colorful beads looked like candy hanging from the long woven strands. She seldom smiled and then only briefly but when she did, that smile lingered in the air. Mario loved that air.

Yolanda was out of place in the eighth grade. She seemed to know more than the other kids.

Sometimes, when someone found the courage to say hello to her, she'd smile and nod her head. From Yolanda, the greeting somehow meant more than all the words everyone else used.

As the police car with Yolanda in it, disappeared around the corner, Mario ran after it, he ran past his house, and ran until he couldn't breathe. Then he lay down behind some bushes, and he cried until dark.

When he arrived home, his mother asked him if he'd been fighting again. He told her that he hadn't. He told her he had a stomachache and that he didn't want dinner.

Yolanda didn't come to school the next day nor the next either. The cafeteria sounded like a cement mixer as the kids speculated on her crime.

Then the weekend came. Saturday morning he walked to Yolanda's house. Her brother Jerome was sitting on the railing of their front porch. He was tough and two years older than Mario. He belonged to a gang and people said he was selling drugs. Everyone called him J.C.. Mario stood on the sidewalk in front of the house.

"Hey little man, what's happnin?" J.C. called out.

"Yolanda, is she okay?"

"She's in the house. You want to see her?"

"No!" he said.

J.C. laughed and called: "Landa, there's a white boy here to see you."

Mario wanted to run, but his legs seemed to be asleep. She came outside and down the sidewalk to him, all the while looking directly into his eyes. She took his left hand in hers and covered it with her other hand for a moment. And then she put his hand to the side of her face. She let his hand go then and he thought he heard her say thank you but he wasn't sure. She turned her back to him and started slowly toward the house.

"Why...cops...?" he called out. She turned back to him, smiled, shrugged her shoulders and went into the house.

Monday she was back at school. He saw her in the morning by her locker and at lunchtime she sat alone in the cafeteria. He saw her as soon as he walked in. She wore blue denim overalls over a red T-shirt, and was sitting with her elbows on the table and her head resting in the palms of her hands. He went directly to her.

"Mind if I sit here?" he asked.

"No," she said, watching him.

He put his bag lunch on the table.

"Somethin on your mind?" she asked, looking at her plate.

"Why'd the cops come for you?" he asked. The words came out louder and faster than he intended.

"Doesn't concern you. I know you want to be my friend, but keep it simple."

"You think I can't handle it?" His face felt hot.

She stood up and smiled then. "The day before the police came I was playing hooker."

"You mean hookey," he said, laughing.

She leaned on the back of the chair next to his and put her face close to his ear.

"No. I mean hooker."

He felt himself start to shake as he watched her walk away. He stood, picked up Yolanda's plate and slammed it down on the table, breaking it into dozens of pieces. He noticed a small puddle of blood dripping to the floor from the cut in his hand, as he left the cafeteria. He went out the front entrance of the school and tried to breathe evenly. He stood with his back against the warm brick, and taking big gasps of air.

The back-to-class bell rang and Mario let his shaky knees bend until his buttocks touched the concrete of the top step. He sat with his back to the wall and remembered all that he could about Yolanda; he remembered the feel of her skin the day, outside her house, when she put his hand to her face. He imagined the sound of her voice and what she would say if they were sitting next to each other. He would ask her questions that would help him understand how a girl the same age as he was could turn tricks, and she would be patient with him, and explain until he did. He would accept her explanations and he would hold her hand in his, and forgive her but make her promise to not play hooker anymore. She would be grateful and hug and kiss him and tell him that she had not realized how much her honor meant to him and that she would never hurt him again.

That day, after school, Mario watched as a long burgundy Cadillac convertible stopped at the corner and waited while Yolanda got in. He was a block away from them and he shouted her name as he watched. The kids closest to where he stood stared at him when he ran down the steps of the entrance to the school, dropping his backpack behind him. He bent in the front lawn area, picked up a rock, and flung it as far as he could after the Cadillac. Neither the driver nor Yolanda noticed Mario, standing in the middle of the street, rubbing the cut in his hand as the Cadillac drove away.

4

The Things You Love

_____

When I first met her, I was seven years old and she was fourteen. I was afraid of her because she was big and black and powerful in every way. My Papa always said bad things about black people, and he taught me to think I was superior to them and to never trust them. When I was nine, I started to attend the church where she sang.

She had the voice of an Angel. That's what everyone at the 2nd Calvary Baptist Church said about Maxine Patterson. They were right. She looked like an Angel too. She had cute dimples that were showing even when she wasn't smiling, and a big beautiful space between her front teeth. She wore her hair short and frizzy and her coffee colored skin was always shiny like she just stepped out of a bath. She was sixteen by then, and when I fell in love with her, I loved everything about her. Whenever we made eye contact in church, she'd come over to me and grab my hand.

"Hey white chocolate, how's my main man?" and I'd be so proud and gushy I couldn't say anything. When the organ would start playing, she'd stand out front in her burgundy robe and make the rafters of that old wood frame church jump for joy. Then, after the sermon and the music and the testifying, I'd go to where she was and wait until she saw me among all her admirers. When she did, she'd wave me over and introduce me as her kid brother. Everybody's eyebrows would raise way up.

She came into my father`s store one day while I was there and she asked to see the cameras.

"What kind are you looking for? We have a lot of cameras." He was reading a book about guns and he didn't look up as he spoke to her, which wasn't hard for me to understand since he loved guns and he hated black people. Maxine saw me over in the corner and her dimples became very deep.

"Howdy friend." She was beaming at me.

"Hello Maxine." I looked over at my Father but I couldn't tell what he was thinking.

"Papa, can I show her the cameras?" He looked at me squinty eyed for a moment.

"Sure, why not? It's about time you learned something anyway."

She and I walked over to the camera section.

"Whew, your father is one scary cracker honey." I showed her the cameras and she picked one out that cost twenty-four dollars. I thought it was a lot of money and I told her so in a whisper.

"The price seems just fine. I'll take it," she said in a loud voice.

The following Sunday, she sat in a swing that hung in a tree in front of the church. She sat me in her lap while a friend of hers took our picture with her new camera.

"When you see that picture sweetly," she said in my ear, "you'll understand why no price is too high for the things you love."

When I got home that afternoon, Papa was

laying on the kitchen floor. His eyes were open, but he wasn't breathing.

"Dad?" I said, "Dad, you okay?" He never played around like I heard of other fathers doing, so I knew it was no joke. I called 911.

"Is he breathing?" the lady asked.

"No, he's not breathing," I said.

"How old are you, honey?" she asked.

"Nine," I said.

"Well, you sound like a brave young man." She told me to try to stay calm and to wait for the help she was sending. What seemed like a long time afterward, I watched as an ambulance slowly drove up to the front of the house, no sirens, lights, nothing. Two guys wearing white jackets walked up to our front door and knocked lightly. I let them in, showed them where my father was laying, and they felt his wrist and his neck.

The doctors said it was a heart attack, and the police called my only living relative, my Aunt Dottie. She came that same night and packed my suitcase and took me to her home, fifty-four miles away. A week later an old beat up pick up truck pulled to the front of Aunt Dottie's house and I watched through the living room window as

Maxine got out and walked up the walkway to our front door. My heart was beating fast as I ran to meet her at the door.

"What you want?" I heard my Aunt Dottie say through the locked screen. I tried to step around my Aunt Dottie's big body so I could see Maxine but my Aunt's arm shot out and held me from getting any closer to the door.

"Afternoon Ma'am," I heard Maxine say softly. "I heard a young friend of mine is staying with you, and I wondered if I might just say hello to him and give him this here pecan pie I made."

"Ain't nobody living here that you would know," my Aunt Dottie said, "so you best be moving on." I went back to the living room window and watched as Maxine walked back to the truck and I cried as the truck pulled from the curb.

Losing Papa scared me, but not being able to see Maxine was different. I longed for her like I never longed for anybody before or since.

Maxine didn't try to see me again, but three years later, when I came home from school one day, there was a letter for me, with my name on it in the mail box. I opened it quickly.

My Dear White Chocolate,

Been a long time. You must be almost a man by now. Here's that picture I promised you. Always remember that no price is too high for the things you love.

Maxine

5

Barb

As I was driving along the coastline, on my way to L.A. from my home in Marin, I saw a young lady of perhaps eighteen years old hitchhiking. Her hair was sun-bleached and she wore a white blouse tied at the midriff, tennys without socks, and bluejean cutoffs.

I pulled over fifteen or so feet ahead of her and waited as she walked quickly to the car. When she arrived, I noticed, through the opened passenger window, as she reached for the door handle, a small white scar across the underside of her left wrist.

"Nice car," she said, as she opened the door and squeaked into the leather seat.

"Where are you heading?" I asked as I pulled from the shoulder onto the highway.

"Depends," she said. Her eyes were studying me carefully.

"On what?" I asked.

"On you," she said.

"How do you mean?"

"Well," she said, "you can pull over, give me your wallet, get out of the car and let me leave for my destination, or you can be stupid, in which case I might end up in jail for murder." When I looked quickly in her direction, I saw the muzzle of a small hand gun. I stepped on the accelerator as hard as I could and the car responded immediately. We were doing ninety, and I was zigging in and out of what few cars were on the highway.

"Pull over," she shouted, jamming the gun into my ribs. I turned the car to the shoulder and pushed the brake pedal with both feet and the car went into a violent spin that didn't stop for what seemed like an hour. I pulled the gun from her hand, and she began to cry.

"Calm down," I said.

We were facing the wrong way on the highway, but still on the shoulder. Passersby were rubbernecking and suddenly a C.H.P. Officer was parked next to us with his lights flashing. I leaned forward and tucked the tiny gun into my shoe before he came to the car.

"Let me do the talking," I said to her.

"You folks all right?" he asked, stepping to the car.

"Yes officer, we're fine," I said. "Did that dog make it?"

"You were avoiding a dog?"

"Yes sir, I must have over-corrected."

"Can I see your driver's license please?" I handed him my license and he studied my face for a moment before handing it back.

"Are you okay Miss?" he asked, scrutinizing her face. She began to cry again, and she pointed at my shoe.

"He has a gun," she shouted and jumped out of the car and ran away from us. The police officer pointed his gun at me.

"Keep your hands where I can see them, and step out of the car," he said.

"Officer, I can explain this." I said, as I got out of the car.

"Put your hands on the hood and spread your legs wide," he said. He took the gun from my shoe and read me my rights before handcuffing me, putting me in the backseat of his squad car and calling for backup.

Lucky for me, they couldn't find the girl and the gun, as it turned out, was a toy.

A week and a half later I was in East L.A. at a flea market, shopping for a gift for a friend, when a shock of sun bleached hair caught my attention. I knew immediately it was her without even looking directly at her. At first my reaction to seeing her suddenly like that I was unnerved because I had been thinking about our encounter quite a bit and going over in my mind the kinds of things I would say to her.

"Remember me?" I said, suddenly standing next to her.

For the briefest second she reacted with the response I expected, but in the same instant she took a step back and began a loud tirade at me in Spanish. People began to stare at us as she continued to holler at me in what probably was

perfect Spanish, and then some of them began to
form a circle around us. I looked at the faces of
those who were closing in on us and they looked
angry and menacing.

"Wait a minute!" I shouted. "What's she
saying?"

A burly man stepped out of the growing circle of
onlookers.

"She said you are a pervert and a child molester,
signor. She said you molested her twelve year old
brother and the police are still looking for you."

"None of that is true!" I shouted, and I reached
out to grab her. Hands grabbed me from every
direction and an elderly woman hit me in the face
with a bag of tortillas.

The girl evaporated into the crowd as a circle
of hands held me in place. Then I watched as a
man pushed his way through the circle and stood
in front of me. He spoke Spanish to them, and I
later learned from a woman standing near me that
he told them that the girl was a con artist, that she
was a gringa who spoke Spanish, and that she had
embezzled thousands of dollars from his brother's
import business.

Slowly, the circle dispersed, and I was left

standing alone as if nothing happened. The next time I saw her, I was on my way home to Marin. It was a beautiful day to travel the coast, and I had finally stopped obsessing on avenging my damaged pride.

She was sitting on a guardrail next to the highway with her arm extended and her thumb held out.

I pulled over to the shoulder of the highway.

"Where are you headed?" she asked as she arrived at the car.

"Bay area," I said.

"Don't I know you?" she asked, taking the front seat.

I was certain she was playing some sort of game, but I played along.

"Yes you look familiar too," I said.

"Do you live in L.A.?" she asked, studying me.

"Nope, bay area," I said.

"I have a twin sister who lives in Oakland," she said.

"Identical?" I asked, looking at her.

"Well, that's what they call us, but we're not identical at all. She's much prettier than I am, and she has a different- temperament."

I looked for some sign of insincerity in her tone and face, but could detect none.

"What's your sister's name?" I asked.

"Barb, we call her, but it's Barbara," she answered without hesitation.

"Mind if I turn on the radio?" she asked.

I shook my head and she promptly found a classical station.

"What's your name?" she asked when the piece had ended.

"Marcus," I said.

"Pleased to meet you," she said, holding out her hand to shake. "My name is Beverly."

Something about her calm demeanor made me begin to wonder if perhaps she was actually telling me the truth.

"Do you travel this highway much?" I asked.

"This is the first time in over a year," she said.

"Do you speak Spanish?" I asked. She squinted at me.

"Un poquito," she said. It sounded quite clumsy, unlike the Spanish spoken by the girl at the flea market in east L.A. "Why? Are you Latino?"

"No," I said. "It's just that I met a girl who looked like you who spoke excellent Spanish.

"I bet you met Barb," she said. "She lived in Mexico for three years and, she speaks fluent Spanish."

"Was she in L.A. a month or so ago?" I asked.

"Yes she was, actually. Our cousin Mickey got married and she came down for the wedding."

"Do you know if she was in east L.A.?"

"Oh sure- I mean that was probably where she stayed."

I thought about how sweet this young woman seemed and how different she was from her sister.

"It's actually hard to imagine you're related to the girl I met, even though you look quite similar." I said.

"Yeah we get that a lot, but Barb has had a rough life," she said.

"Didn't you grow up together?" I asked.

"No- We were put up for adoption when we were two years old, and we went to separate homes." She looked thoughtful and became silent for awhile, and I sensed she didn't want to talk. I wanted to know more, but it didn't seem like the right time to pursue the subject.

"Can we make a rest stop?" she asked, pointing

at a gas station/mini mart a short distance ahead of us.

I nodded and pulled into the parking lot. We went to the restrooms, and I came out first and sat in the car and waited. She came out moments after me, carrying two coffees.

"Do you take cream?" she asked as she arrived at the car.

"Yes," I said. She opened the lid to one of the coffees and added one cream.

We drank our coffees without saying anything.

"Do you mind if I call you Mark?" she asked. I shook my head.

"Are you and your sister close?" I asked as I started the car.

"We're like one person sometimes," she said.

"The girl I met in east L.A. seemed very difficult," I said

"I get like that too sometimes," she said. "Don't you?"

"Do you live in L.A.?" I asked. She nodded.

"Are you going to visit your sister?"

"Yes," she said. "I haven't seen her since the wedding."

We talked about favorite foods and music, the

silliness of worshipping celebrities, Philosophy and art. The time passed quickly, and before we knew it, I was dropping her off.

"Thanks," she said, reaching out her left hand to shake mine. I took her hand in mine and turned it as she opened the door with her right. There, on her left wrist, was the same small white scar. We made eye contact on her way out the door, and she smiled faintly.

6

Kathy Quinn

The pavement was cold beneath my back. Even though he had thrown me to the ground, his hands were still twisted in my shirt. Then his knees came crashing into my stomach, and I lost my breath for a moment. I looked up into his toothless smile as he smashed his fist to the side of my head. I immediately felt the swelling begin.

"Give up?" Bob Lancaster hollered into my face.

I shook my head no, and he punched me again, bloodying my nose.

"Give up?" He was getting louder as a crowd

gathered. He was a big kid, much taller and heavier than I was. He looked like a big farm boy transplanted into the city. Although I hadn't given him much of a fight, he was breathing heavily as though I had given him a real battle.

My face was cut and swelling, and I could taste my own blood. As I looked around the gathering group of kids, I noticed Kathy Quinn crying. She wasn't looking at us; I couldn't see her eyes, just the motion of her long flaxen hair as her body shook as she sobbed. She and I were in the same eighth grade class, and each day we had lunch at the same table in the cafeteria.

"Yuck, peanut butter," I'd say.

"Mmmm, I love peanut butter. I'll give you half a baloney sandwich and a banana for your peanut butter," she'd say.

"Only if you'll take an apple too," I'd respond.

And then she'd smile, and her smile started in her eyes and spread over her whole face. I did everything I could think of to make her smile every day.

"Give up, weeney?"

"No! Do you?" The blood from my mouth

splattered onto his face when I spoke, and I heard the waver in my voice.

A car stopped and a chubby man with a red nose and a cigar got out.

"You kids cut that out. Go on, break it up, all of you, or I'll call a cop."

"We'll finish this later, puke face," Bob called to me over his shoulder as he walked away.

In school the next day, while I was in line for gym class, Bob walked by me, punched the palm of his hand with his fist, sneered at me, and pointed at the entrance to school. I felt a queasiness begin in my stomach and spread to a shakiness in my legs. Kathy and I didn't have lunch together that day. I saw her sitting at a table with some kids, but I didn't sit with them. I sat alone at a corner table where I could see who came and who left.

When the dismissal bell rang that day, it reminded me of Bob, and I was tense and scared as I walked down the seven concrete steps at the school entrance. He grabbed my shoulder from behind, spun me around, and pushed me. I extended my arms behind me to keep my balance, dropping my books on the ground. He and two of his buddies laughed at me, and then I heard Kathy's voice from the steps behind me:

"Why don't you pick on someone your own size?"

"Why? You like this little sissy?" he said walking to me as I knelt in the lawn, picking up my books. I was kneeling, and he slapped me on the back of my head.

"Cut it out!" she shouted.

He laughed and knocked me over with his knee. "Excuse me," he said with a smirk. He and his friends walked away then, and Kathy knelt next to me, helping me gather my things.

"Thanks," I said.

She smiled. "Are you goin' to Maryanne's birthday party tomorrow night?" she asked. I shrugged my shoulders. "You're invited, if you want to go, because I'm supposed to invite anybody I want to go with, and you're who I want to go with."

"Really?" I said.?She nodded and handed me my books as we both stood. "Sure," I said.?"See ya at my house at seven then?" she asked. I nodded as she got into her mother's car, which was waiting at the curb.

That Saturday evening at Maryanne's party, Kathy and I sat alone in the living room while all the other kids ate birthday cake in the dining room.

"Wanna go steady with me?" I asked. She nodded and kissed me. I didn't have a ring to give her so I gave her my St. Christopher medal, which was supposed to protect all travelers. She put the chain around her neck and turned her back to me so that I could close the clasp. After I closed it, she turned to me and looked very seriously into my eyes.

"Don't ever stoop to Bob's level," she said. I didn't know what to say. I felt my face flush, and I could feel a knot of tension develop in the back of my neck.

Later that evening, when I kissed her good night in front of her house, she held my hand.

"You're different than the other boys. You don't think you have to be a jerk just because somebody else is acting like one," she said. I knew she meant Bob again, and I wanted her to know that I would have loved to kick the stuffing out of him if I thought I had a chance. Instead I kissed her lips and said goodnight.

At school on Monday before the commencement bell, I was drinking water from the fountain when someone shoved me sideways. When I regained my balance, Bob was drinking and looking up at me with a sneer.

That afternoon, as Kathy and I were having lunch, Bob came to our table with two of his friends.

"You girls need to go to a different table. This table is for boys only." I felt my face flush and grow extremely hot. "You better get out of here," Kathy said, "or I'm going to tell the cafeteria monitor."?Bob was holding a tray with his lunch and a glass of water on it; he balanced the tray with one hand and knocked the glass of water over with the other, flinging it sideways onto Kathy.

Before I could think, I lunged at Bob and stabbed him in the shoulder with my fork, and while he stood in shock from the pain and the suddenness of my attack, I punched him with a barrage of punches that sent him to his back on the floor. I immediately jumped on top of him and kept hitting him until an adult pulled me from him. I struggled free from the adult, grabbed a cafeteria chair, and raised it over my head, but another adult pulled it from me before I could smash Bob with it. The cafeteria was silent, and almost everyone stood in a circle around us. Bob was lying on his back, his face all bloody, and the fork was still in his shoulder.

Matty Rendazzo called out that I was having Bob for lunch, and everyone laughed, everyone except Kathy. She walked up to me with her hands behind her neck, and put her face close to mine. "I thought you were different," she whispered as she put my St. Christopher medal in my shirt pocket and walked away and out of the cafeteria. I wanted to call her back or run after her, but I just stood amidst a mixture of human voices that sounded like a huge orchestra tuning up. As my mind raced through the entire event that had just happened, I looked for what I could have done differently.

Days later, after a short suspension from school, a heavy verbal reprimand from the principal, and two sessions with the school counselor, the drama had diminished. Bob had been reported to the school authorities for being a bully many times before and, because of that, I was not expelled.

I rode my bike to Kathy's house late one weekend morning and, while I stood on her front porch, her mother's car pulled into the driveway, and Kathy and her mother got out with grocery bags. I went and grabbed two bags and carried them to the door, and her mother invited me in.

"Would you like a glass of orange juice or milk?" her mother asked. I shook my head no and looked at Kathy. Her mother smiled and left the room.

"Can we talk?" I asked.

"Not much to say," she said, looking away from me.

"I got mad because he spilt water on you," I said.

"I know," she said, as she walked across the room from me and sat in a chair.

"I still like you," I said.

"Doesn't matter anymore." Her voice sounded flat, like she was tired of talking to me.

"Can I have another chance?" She shook her head no and left the room. I stood alone in the middle of her living room, studied the chair where she had been sitting, took my St. Christopher medal from around my neck, placed it on the coffee table, and was just about to leave, when a car screeched into the driveway. It sounded as if it had been going too fast. A moment later I heard a man's voice.

"Whose Goddamned bicycle is that on the lawn?"

"Sshh Tom, it's Kathy's friend and he'll hear you," I heard her mother plead. She stood in the doorway with her back to me. I saw his hand on her shoulder and then she tumbled backwards into the wall as he pushed her.

"You've been drinking again, haven't you?" Her voice was wavering. Kathy came out of a room, stood by her door, and watched.

"Is that your sorry-ass bike on my lawn?" he asked me. He was a big man with a red, angry looking face.

I nodded.

"You get the hell out of my house, get that bike off my lawn, and don't come back here no more, you hear?" I turned my back to him, walked out the front door, got on my bike and rode home.

That night, I had trouble sleeping as I thought about Kathy and her family. I thought about how I must have looked to Kathy when I stabbed Bob with the fork. I lay there wishing there were something I could do or say that would wipe away her memory of the fight. I understood, for the first time, that I responded to Bob in exactly the way that would push her from me. I understood that from her point of view, there could never be a justification for violence and that if I wanted to be her friend, I'd have to find some other way to respond to the Bobs of this world than with rage.

Monday, at school, when I went into the cafeteria at lunch time, I saw Kathy sitting at our table. She had her hair back in a pony tail, and she was wearing her red corduroy dress, which she knew was my favorite because I had told her. She smiled as I approached her table.

"Sorry," I said.

"Me too,"she said. I sat down next to her and when I looked at her, I saw she was wearing my medal.

"I've decided to never act crazy like that again," I said as I looked down at the table.

"If you keep your word, I'll be your girl," she said.

7

Marilyn Monroe

I was almost comatose, just came out of surgery and when I woke up, someone was holding my hand and stroking it. I opened my eyes and a beautiful blonde woman was sitting in a chair next to the bed and had my hand in both of hers. As my vision cleared, it became clear to me that the woman was Marilyn Monroe. I rubbed my eyes with my free hand to clear them.

"Marilyn?" I said.

"Hello," she said in her throaty, most sultry voice.

She was ten times more beautiful than I remembered from the movies.

"It's so good to see you," I said. She smiled and began to hum. I loved her sound; it was so comforting.

"Well," she said, "I wanted you to know that I care about you."

Just then, my wife walked in, and Marilyn disappeared.

"Did you see her?" I asked, much like a child on Christmas morning.

"See who?" my wife asked.

"Marilyn" I said, louder than I intended.

"Marilyn?" she said. "Marilyn who?

"Marilyn Monroe," I said. "She was just here, holding my hand." The nurse had come in by then, and she and my wife exchanged knowing glances.

"What?" I said. "You don't believe me?"

"She only comes to visit on Tuesdays and Thursdays," the nurse said, " and today is Wednesday." I looked at my wife, and she was laughing.

"So nobody believes me," I said, pouting a bit.

A doctor came in to check on me and as he listened to my heart, the nurse stood by him.

"This patient had a visitor today," she said.

"Oh?" he said. "Someone significant?" he said with a grin and a wink.

"Marilyn Monroe," she said, holding back a laugh.

"Wow," he said, "I haven't seen her in a while. I wish I had been here." By now a number of the hospital staff were in on what seemed to be a joke.

"Is she as pretty in person?" One orderly asked after the doctor had gone.

"The next time she visits, can you get me an autograph?" a male nurse called to me as he passed.

This went on for days as I recovered. Then, on the day I was to be discharged, I was alone in my room, waiting for my wife to come and pick me up, and in walked Marilyn again. She came close to my bed and took my hand in hers.

"I heard you were leaving today," she said. "I just had to say goodbye." I was choked up. She leaned over me and brought her face close to mine, and she kissed me on my mouth. It was such a gentle, sensuous kiss I began to doubt it actually happened.

She disappeared as my wife approached. My wife was frowning.

"Who kissed you?" she asked as she took a hanky from her purse and rubbed the lipstick off my lips.

8

Maudie Parks

———————

Maudie Parks rode the bus every Sunday morning to the huge Baptist tent on Lexington Avenue in Corliss Park. She took the 7 o'clock bus because she wanted to be sure to get there before the singing started. 'There was nothing on earth could bring a body closer to God than voices lifted up in harmony' was what she always said.

She especially liked the 7A bus because it brought her right to the flapped-over entrance to the tent. The 10E brought her to Lexington Avenue, but it turned on Park, three blocks before the tent, and her tired old arthritic legs made her wait for the 7A even though the 10E ran more often.

So she waited that Sunday morning, just as she had every Sunday morning for the previous twenty-two years. It was a particularly cold morning, and her arthritis was aching even as she sat. An old white man was sitting at the bus stop when she got there that morning, and even though she didn't usually talk to white folk, he said hello so she said hello back. She noticed, through the corner of her eye, that a cane was leaning on the bench next to his leg. She thought to herself that a cane wouldn't be a bad idea for herself as well. She was going to stand and wait but her legs ached so and though she didn't fancy sitting on the same bench as a strange white man, he was sitting all the way at one end, so she sat at the other.

"It sure is a cold morning," he said, a puff of smoke from the cold coming out of his mouth as he spoke.

"Coldest one so far," she said.

"It must be about 10 or 15 degrees," he said.

"Definitely freezing," she said.

"You taking the 10E?" he asked.

"7A," she said.

"Does that get you to Lexington?" he asked.

"Yep, right to Corliss Park," she said.

"Corliss Park? Why, that's where I'm going," he said.

"Well the 10E will get you close, but the 7A will take you right to it," she said.

Maudie wondered why this old white man was going to Corliss Park, since everybody knew it was a rundown park in the middle of the ghetto, but she wasn't curious enough to ask a white person a personal question.

"If I take the 7A, would you mind telling me when we get to Corliss Park?" he asked. She thought it was kind of an odd request since there was no way he wouldn't be able to tell when they arrived at Corliss Park, but she agreed.

"Sure," she said.

"My name is Thomas," he said as he leaned toward her and held out his hand. She took his hand and shook it.

"Maudie," she said, all the while thinking he was the oddest duck she had ever met.

Two 10E buses came and went before a 7A arrived, but they both waited patiently. He took her arm when she got up to get on the bus, and they took a seat together. She looked around at the others on the bus; most of them were people she knew who were regular early-Sunday-morning bus riders. She felt a little embarrassed about getting on her bus with a white man and then sitting with him. They rode in silence for a while.

"You ride this bus often?" he asked suddenly. She had been looking out the window and thinking that the sky looked like it might snow.

"Every Sunday morning," she said.

"You must know every stop and many of the people who ride with you," he said.

"Yeah, I guess I do," she said.

They didn't speak again until they reached the tent on Lexington Avenue. The tent was situated at the entrance to Corliss Park.

"This is it," she said, thinking she was stating the obvious.

"Ahh, good, good, and where is the tent where the beautiful singing takes place?" he asked. She looked at him.

"The tent is right in front of you. What are you-blind?" she said it without thinking.

"Yes," he said, "I am." She felt stupid, and she grabbed his hand.

"Come with me," she said, "that's where I'm going too."

As they entered the flapped-over entrance together, an organ played softly in the background. Numerous friends of Maudie's greeted her as she and her companion passed through the rows of people seated in folding chairs. She found two empty folding chairs and, seating him first, she took the seat beside him.

The minister stepped up to the pulpit and spoke about forgiveness and healing. It was an inspiring sermon, and the singing that followed began softly, as if the congregation was so moved that they could not at first remove themselves from the spell-like substance of the words. Slowly, though, the congregation began to sing out, and the quality of the voices was rich and beautiful. Even after so many years of singing these songs, Maudie held the book of psalms before her and read as she sang. She held the book for her companion to read, and then, remembering that he couldn't see, she turned to him. He had his eyes closed, and he was singing. He sang every word correctly, and his voice was rich and deep and in perfect pitch with the congregation. Maudie kept staring at him, amazed at how perfectly he sang every word and at how beautiful his face had become.

Maudie believed that almost everything that happened to people was accidental, but that interspersed with all of these accidental happenings there were what she liked to call events. Events, unlike accidental happenings, were intentionally woven patterns in our lives, a part of our destiny. She believed now, as she watched this old white man sing, that he was a part of her destiny. There seemed to be nothing about him that she could predict. Accidental happenings were predictable in their lack of reliability; everything about this white man that she was able to observe was that he was reliable, but only in retrospect and therefore unpredictable. She began to like him, and it frightened her because every white person she had ever liked had hurt her.

When the services ended and the people began to file out of the tent, the white man reached for her hand. She took it and squeezed gently.

"I got you," she said, and he squeezed back.

"Thank you," he said.

"For what?" she asked.

"For helping me get here," he said, "and for being kind to a stranger."

"Well you sure didn't put me out any," she said, "I was coming here anyway."

"Would you like to have a cup of coffee with me?" he asked. Maudie stiffened at the thought. The only place close that she knew about was Coffee Jones, and she hardly felt safe going there herself; going with a white man seemed foolhardy.

"Uh, my legs are aching from the cold, and I think I best be getting home now," she said. She looked at him after she had spoken, and he looked so disappointed that she quickly added: "How about I fix us a fresh pot at my house; it's close to where we caught the bus."

"Well if you're sure it's no problem," he said, "I'd be honored to have a cup of coffee at your home."

They caught the bus almost immediately after stepping out of the tent, and they were soon standing at the bus stop where they had met. He had her arm, and they began walking the half block to her home.

"Where you live?" she asked as they approached her house.

"1407 Magellan," he said. "I moved in with my grand daughter yesterday."

"This is 1403 Magellan," she said, "You live two houses down?" He looked puzzled.

"I don't know," he said. "Sure seems lucky if I do."

They stood on her porch and she reached into her purse for her key just as the door opened and her daughter, Shanika stood in front of her.

"Hello baby, what you doing here?" Maudie asked. Shanika didn't answer but looked from the strange white man back to Maudie. Her face was battered and bruised.

"Who's this?" she asked.

"This is—this is–What's your name again?" she asked.

"Thomas," he said, reaching out his hand in the wrong direction, "and I'm pleased to meet you."

"This is my youngest daughter Shanika," Maudie said. Then Maudie noticed her daughter's face. "What happened to you?" she asked. Shanika's left eye was swollen.

"Nothing I care to talk about right now," she said, staring at the white man.

"He didn't hit you, did he?" Maudie hollered.

"Mama, I do not want to talk about this right now," she said.

"Talk hell," Maudie said. "He's not getting away with it," "not again."

"Let me handle it," Shanika said.

"I don't like the way you're handling it," she said. "Where is the baby?"

"At Tonisha's," she said. "Mama, I already been through hell last night. Please don't make me sorry I came here." Maudie went into the kitchen, leaving Shanika and the white man standing in the middle of the livingroom. They heard her making coffee, and Shanika left him and went into the kitchen. Their voices could be heard as Maudie told Shanika that he was blind and would she please show him to a seat while she made coffee. Shanika came back into the room and, taking his arm, she led him to the sofa and sat him down.

"I hope you understand that our problems are not about you, Mister," she said.

"Thomas," he said, correcting her use of Mister. "About me? Why would they be about me?"

"I just want to make sure that you're not one of those white guys who thinks that every time a person of color has a problem it's because of something they should or shouldn't have done," she said. Thomas looked very solemn and said nothing for a moment, and then he began laughing. The laughing began with a light chuckle and grew into a belly laugh.

"Look at me, Shanika," he said. "Do I look like I'm going to assume guilt about somebody else's problems?"

"No," she said, "I guess not. How you know my Mama?"

"She helped me get to Sunday services this morning," he said.

"Sunday services? What Sunday services?" she asked.

"The same Sunday services your mother goes to," he said.

"You went to Corliss Park?"

"That's right," he said. "Your mama and I took the bus together."

"But those services are for black folk," she said.

"Well, blame my failing to notice on my lack of sight," he said.

"Weren't you afraid?" she asked.

"Of what?"

"Of being the only white person," she said.

"Close your eyes," he said. "What do you see?"

"Nothing."

"Right," he said. "How can a reasonable person be afraid of nothing?"

"Not seeing something isn't the same as it not existing," she said.

"I think reality is in the head," he said.

"You think our reality is in our heads?" she asked.

"Yeah," he said. "I do."

"What the hell does that mean?" she asked. He smiled as he heard Maudie enter the room.

"All we can control is our responses," he said. "Instead of getting mad and hating someone when we feel wronged, we can turn that feeling into profit."

"Profit?!," Shanika almost shouted. "How do I profit from getting beat-up by my nasty-ass old man?"

Maudie put the mug of coffee in his hand.

"Milk?" she asked. He shook his head. Shanika had been standing the whole time and now she sat by her mother on the sofa.

"I came in on the tail end of your conversation," Maudie said. "What were you saying about profit?"

"Shanika was just asking me about our morning together," he said, "and somehow we got into a philosophical discussion on perspectives."

"Thomas thinks we create our own reality," Shanika said, "right Thomas? We can make everything beautiful, and we can love everybody. Right Thomas?" She got louder as she spoke. Maudie grabbed Shanika's arm and squeezed it tight, but said nothing to her.

"Sounds like something Dr. King might say," Maudie said.

"It's not a new concept," Thomas said. "James Baldwin, Ralph Ellison, Richard Wright, and many others who've known oppression have spoken eloquently about using their suffering as a fuel to propel and motivate them."

"I guess," Shanika said, "it's easy to talk about profiting from getting knocked around when you're a blind white man."

"Shanika!" Maudie shouted. Thomas held up his hand.

"That's quite understandable," he said. "But how much suffering does a person need to go through in order to understand the idea that we can grow from harships? Taking in what we find unbearable and using it the right way, makes us wiser."

"How am I going to use my frustrated, abusive, out-of-work, ex-con husband, who is the father of my three hungry children, Mr. Thomas- Can you answer me that?" Shanika asked.

"You can't use him for anything," he said. "What you use are your feelings about the situation."

"Tell me something Doctor 'Love and Beauty–"

"Hold it there," Maudie shouted. "Don't you be laying your heaviness and self-pity at this man's feet like he's responsible for everything that's going wrong with your life. Why are you blaming him? All he's doing is trying to offer you some good advice."

"I don't need advice from a self-righteous white man who probably never went a day hungry in his life," she said. I didn't ask for his advice, and I don't want it." Shanika stood up, grabbed her jacket and ran out the door.

"Sorry," he said.

"She's just a mess right now," Maudie said. "She got involved with a gangster, and she's stuck with him."

"Sorry to hear that," he said. "Sometimes we can only wait and watch."

"I'm getting better at letting her figure things out for herself. It's her kids that make it the hardest for me. Would you like some more coffee?" she asked.

"Yes I would," he said. She left the room and returned with the pot, and after filling their cups, she placed the pot on a pot holder which she first placed on the coffee table. As she placed the pot on the coffee table her face came very close to his, and he leaned forward and kissed her on the corner of her mouth. Shocked, she jolted back and stared at him.

"I hope that was an accident," she said.

"Missing your lips was," he said.

She was confused and angry as the door came flying open and Rasheed, her son-in-law, stood in the middle of the living room staring at them.

"Where is she? he shouted.

"You got no business barging into my house," Maudie hollered.

"Where's my wife?" he hollered back.

"Why don't you settle down, son?" Thomas said, as he stood up.

"Who's this white guy?" the young man snarled at her.

"That's none of your business," she said. "Now get out of my house before I call the police."

"I'll go after you tell me where she is," he said. "Is she here?" he shouted looking all around.

Maudie went to the phone and picked up the headset and Rasheed covered the five feet between them in one step and, swinging his arm, hit her across the wrist, sending the phone flying.

Thomas took a step in their direction, and Rasheed rushed to him and punched him in the jaw, knocking him to the floor. Maudie screamed.

"You fool," she shouted. "He's blind!" She ran to Thomas and cradled his head in her lap as he lay on the floor.

Rasheed ran from the house, and they heard an engine rev and then wheels peeling out.

"Welcome to my world," she said as she caressed his forehead. "You okay?"

"Yes," he said. And then, after a moment of silence, he asked, "Can I touch your face?" She stood him up without answering, led him to the sofa, sat him down, and sat still next to him while he ran his fingers over first the outline of her face and then each line and crevice of her features. When he was finished, he rested his head in her lap and said nothing.

"How did my face feel?" she asked.

"You're a keeper," he said. And he fell asleep while she stroked his temples.

After awhile, Maudie carefully slid her legs out from under the old man's head and left him sleeping. She took the coffee mugs and coffee pot to the kitchen and did house hold things. As she quietly and methodically did her chores, she thought about the man sleeping on her sofa. Since meeting him, the feeling never left her that he was a significant event in her life, and that it was no accident that they had met. She felt as if she had known him all of her life, like he had somehow played a part in all that she understood and had come to believe about people and ideas. She knew, without ever having spoken about it with him, that he understood justice in a different way than every other white person that she had ever met.

"Maudie," she heard him call from the living room.

"Yes?" she asked, coming to the living room archway.

"What time is it?" he asked. She looked at the clock in the kitchen.

"One ten," she said. He stood up, patted out the wrinkles in his clothing, and grabbed his cane.

"I best be going," he said, "before my grand daughter starts to worry."

"Let me grab my coat, and I'll walk you there," she said.

Moments later, as they stood in front of his grand daughter's home, they embraced as she took his hand in hers, she kissed him lightly on his lips.

9

Thanks For Nothing

———————

One day I found the following ad on Craigslist: Help needed- 70 year old man, flat tire, no spare, broke, hungry, out of work, no family, needs help. I have nothing to offer in exchange for a tire and a slice of bread. If this sounds like something you'd be willing to do, you can find me in my 1990 blue ford on citrus lane; just knock on the window if I'm asleep. Thank you and have a good day.

So, being the sort of fellow who is inclined to explore situations that might yield the unusual, I went to find the author of this notice, and here is my story.

I found the blue Ford, which had a flat tire, and a very thin man with wispy gray hair sitting behind the steering wheel with his head leaning against the window. His hair, what there was of it, was long and unkempt, and he had a long white beard that looked wind blown. He was asleep, so I knocked on the window. He looked abruptly at me with intense green eyes. There was no discernible emotion in his eyes, only the look of a man who had come to a full stop, both literally and figuratively. He rolled down his window, and before I could speak, he handed me a piece of paper through the opened window. I took the paper and read it twice through. It read:

'Before you make any attempt to communicate with me, please be aware that I cannot hear or speak. I have not had anything to eat since Tuesday- it was now Saturday- and the police are telling me that I have until tomorrow to move my car or it will be impounded. If you are answering my ad and wish to offer me help, please bring me a cup of coffee and something to eat.'

I walked immediately to a corner coffee shop and ordered him a cup of coffee and a turkey sandwich. I walked back to where I had left him, and he was outside of his car, sitting on the front fender. He smiled as I approached. Without saying a word, I handed him the coffee and sandwich. He took them with little to no show of emotion. He took the wrapper off of the sandwich and took a bite of it then he opened the coffee and drank. I watched as he slowly ate and drank my offerings.

He looked at me as he finished the last of his coffee, and it appeared that something that had been missing from his eyes was now visible—hope?

I pointed to the flat tire, and he smiled. After investigating the trunk of his car and finding he had neither spare nor jack, I walked to my car and brought back a jack. He loosened the lugs on his flat tire while I placed the jack into position and jacked up his car. He removed the flat, and I placed it into the trunk of my car and brought it to a garage for repair. When I returned with the repaired tire, he handed me a gift-wrapped medium sized cardboard box. The gift wrapping said Happy Birthday on it. It felt light, like maybe it had only paper in it. I started to say something, and then remembered he couldn't hear or speak. The box was taped shut, so I placed it on the ground and proceeded to place the repaired tire onto the drum. He knelt by my side and took over the chore, so I went back to the box and began to open it. The man was old, handicapped, homeless and destitute, so I figured whatever was in the box had to be of value only to him. He stood up and came to me before I could finish opening the box. He put his hand on my arm and motioned me to wait. He took a pen from his shirt pocket and wrote on a scrap of paper would I please not open the box until he had finished changing the tire. I was a little curious, but I motioned okay and I went back to his car with him. After we finished, he sat in his car and watched as I opened the box.

I removed the tape, opened the box and was somewhat surprised to find the box was empty except for an envelope. He was smiling as he watched me look into the box. I smiled back and closed the flaps on the box. I began to open the envelope as I walked back to my car. He blew his horn at me and when I looked back in his direction he waved goodbye, started his car and drove off.

I sat on the hood of my car and opened the envelope:

If you are opening this envelope, you've helped me more than words could express. Thank you. As stated in the Craigslist ad, I don't have any worldly possessions to offer you, so I'm hoping these few words based on my experience might benefit you in some way:

Greed hastens the death of spirit
Always strive to be where you are
Shun praise, as it deludes
Find comfort in silence, for therein lies truth
Give with your heart or not at all
Learn your nature and be true to it
Stay in tune with the rhythm of your being
A humble heart begets a grateful spirit

10

Arnies

———

All Rosey Barrett knew for sure, was that she loved Arnie's Bar and Grill and that even if Mister Shiffler was old and musty looking, at least he was the best damn pool shooter she ever saw. She was sitting at the bar, watching Mister Shiffler run almost every one of the solid balls in the game of eight ball he was playing against a tall skinny guy who was wearing a cowboy hat. She watched intently as Mister Shiffler finished the solids and sank the eight ball. The young man hung his head and handed Mister Shiffler yet another five-dollar bill.

"That's thirty-five dollars. Damn, I'm stupid."

"You almost had me that time," Mister Shiffler said as he put the five dollars in his pocket.

Rosey didn't think so. She watched the whole game, and never once did it seem the skinny cowboy would win. Mister Shiffler turned to Rosey and winked.

"Give Rosey another drink," he hollered to Mat, the bartender. Rosey was proud that Mister Shiffler liked her so much, even if his hands were hard and calloused and sticky and his breath smelled terrible, she liked that he made her feel important here at Arnie's. Later, in the motel across the street, she knew he would touch her again and put his smelly mouth on hers, but right now she felt good. Mat put the vodka orange juice in front of her, and she took a big gulp and watched in the mirror over the bar as the door opened, and a young city-looking man walked in. Rosey had never seen the likes of him. His face was tan and clean shaven, and his short-sleeve shirt fit everywhere except the arms where it was straining to go around his huge muscles.

He stepped up to the bar right next to Rosey, and he was almost touching her.

"Gimme a beah," he said to Mat.

"Huh?" Mat said.

"Don'cha have beah heah?" he said pointing at the beer taps. Mat poured him a beer, and the young man sat down next to Rosey, turned his back to the bar, and watched Mister Shiffler whup Danny Crowder at another game of eight ball. Mister Shiffler put Danny's five dollars on the bar right next to Rosey's drink after the game was over and motioned to Mat to pour her another. The young city guy leaned forward around Rosey and stared at Mister Shiffler.

"Wanna play for another fiver?" he asked.

"Rack'em," Mister Shiffler said.

The young man racked the balls, and Mister Shiffler broke. Rosey had seen Mister Shiffler play many times, but never had she seen him play so well as this game. After the break, he made every one of his balls and just barely missed the eight. Rosey's face felt hot to her, and she got up and went to the lady's room. She put cold water on her face and hurried back to watch the game. Mister

Shiffler was handing the young man five dollars when she stepped out of the lady's room.

"I only made one mistake," he said, "it was playing you in the first place."

Rosey sat down in front of her half-finished drink. She turned and watched as Mister Shiffler bent over to rack the balls. She couldn't ever remember him doing that before. She watched as the young man broke and then ran the entire rack, including the eight ball. Mister Shiffler gave him another five dollars and came over and stood by Rosey.

"Rosey, let's you and me get out of here and find something more interesting to do," he said. Rosey thought his breath smelled worse than it ever did before, and she shook her head no. Mister Shiffler grabbed her wrist with his sticky calloused hand, and Rosey struggled free.

"Bitch," he said as he walked toward the door.

Rosey finished her drink and looked at the young city guy sitting next to her.

"You sure can shoot pool, Mister," she said. He smiled at her.

"Where I'm from, everybody and their granmudder shoots pool."

"Where's that?" she asked

"HobokenNewJersey," he said. Rosey laughed at the funny sounding name.

"What?" he asked, "you been there?" Rosey shook her head no.

"You wannanudder drink?" he asked. Rosey thought for a moment.

"Okay," she said. He ordered a drink for her and a beer for himself.

"What's your name?" he asked.

"Rosey."

"Hey, Rosey, Nick," he said, as he held up his bottle of beer to clink against her glass. Mister Shiffler never did that she thought. "So Rosey, you live aroun' heah?" he made a circular motion with his index finger as he asked. Rosey struggled to translate the words he was saying each time he spoke.

"Uh, no," she said finally. "I live down by the machine shop-it's where I work too."

"I got my ca' outside if you wanna ride somewheas."

Mister Shiffler and her always drove across to the motel in his old Chevy truck, and she wondered what the city guy's car was like.

"How come you call it a ca'? It's car, c-a-r."

"Did you understand?" he asked.

"Yeah, but-"

"I rest my case."?Rosey finished her drink and went to the lady's room. When she returned, the city guy was shooting pool with Danny Stokes while his brothers Bobby and Trevor watched. She felt uneasy as she watched the city guy sink ball after ball. She wanted to warn him to let him know that the Stokes brothers were in and out of jail for fighting most of the time. The city guy finished off Danny easily and collected five dollars from him.

"Where you from Mister?" Bobby called from the barstool he was sitting on.

"Hoboken New Jersey," the city guy said.

"Sounds like a long way from here," Bobby continued. "Your mama know you're so far from home?"

City guy held onto his pool cue, turned his back to Bobby and Trevor, and ordered another drink for Rosey and a beer for himself.

"I asked you a question, boy," Bobby said as he grabbed city guy's arm and spun him to face him. City guy, with one move, used the butt of the pool cue to poke Bobby in the eye and swing around and slam Trevor in the jaw, knocking him off the stool and onto the floor. Danny jumped him from behind, and Rosey broke city guy's beer bottle on Danny's head.

"Thanks," city guy said, and he and Rosey walked outside. She knew his car as soon as she saw the metallic tan color and the New Jersey plates.

"I always liked convertibles," she said, as she slid across the tan leather. She took off her clothes as they entered the motel room and adjusted the shower water. He entered the shower with her. Rosey loved the softness of his hands and his sweet smelling breath. They left the motel at noon the next day.

"You wanna go to Hoboken with me?" he asked.

"Naw, just drop me off at Arnie's," Rosey said.

11

Soup Lady

———————

I woke up coughing last night, just as I had almost every night for the previous three weeks. My doctor said I had pneumonia. Hot from fever then chills, dry hacking cough, headache, I had it all. So, as I lay there, all alone, miserable and wondering if this was the end, I heard a knocking at the door.

I glanced at the alarm clock on my end table as I got out of bed and put on my robe, and it read 11 o'clock. As I approached my front door, I could see by the porch light, through the glass pane of my front door, a matronly woman of perhaps fifty years old, standing there with a huge pot under her arm.

"Hello?" I said as I opened the door part way. She pushed the door the rest of the way open and breezed past me. Surprised by the suddenness of the move and the forcefulness with which she made her way in, I stood gazing at her.

"Who are you," I asked, " and why are you in my house.

"I'm here to make you chicken soup," she called to me as she rushed past me to my kitchen and began to place various items from her pot onto my kitchen table. As she began to fill her pot with water from my tap, I could only stare and wonder. 'Was this woman mad?' 'Should I call the police?'

"Excuse me," I said, "but I didn't order any chicken soup."

"Are you sick?" she called from the kitchen?

"Well, yes," I said.

"So what's your problem with my making chicken soup for you?"

"Well, I don't even know you, for one," I said. It sounded stupid, even to me. I went to the kitchen and watched her. She was suddenly quite beautiful, her hair was long, and she had it tied in a ponytail behind her but flowing over one shoulder across her breast. Her eyes were dark and almost closed as she worked. She had a short round body, not fat, but not thin either. She looked powerful and determined as she prepared all of the ingredients for the soup. She wore what looked like a velvet red apron, and she had the sleeves of her white blouse rolled up past her elbows.

"You can go to bed if you want," she said softly. "I'll call you when it's ready."

"But who are you?" I sounded like a whiney child. "And how did you know I was sick?" She stopped what she was doing and turned to me. She had her hands on her hips.

"Do you want to feel better?"

"Of course," I said. "But..."

"Just let me go about my business, and we'll talk later." It sounded reasonable, and I felt myself drop my insistence that I understand what was happening.

"I'm going to bed," I said as I climbed the steps to my loft.

"Good idea," she said. "I'll let you know when the soup is ready."

Once I was in bed again, I fell to sleep easily, and I felt a calm I hadn't felt in weeks.

When I woke up, she was sitting on the edge of the bed, next to me.

She had a big bowl of soup on her lap, and it smelled heavenly.

"Open up," she said, holding a spoon up to my mouth. I allowed her to feed me the first spoonful.

"It's delicious," I said. "Can I feed myself?"

She laughed and gave me the spoon.

"Now," she said, "I want you to repeat after me"

I had the spoon in my mouth, but I nodded.

"Thank you for this heavenly, life-giving soup," she began.

"Thank you for this heavenly, life-giving soup," I repeated.

"But who am I thanking?" I blurted, breaking the spell she was creating.

"It doesn't matter," she said. "Just look up as you repeat my words."

"I will forever more remember to be grateful for all the good things bestowed upon me and try to never question their origin or motives again," she continued, and I repeated.

When I finished the entire bowl, I closed my

eyes, and I felt a light kiss on my forehead. I woke up hours later and looked around the room. I felt better than I had in a very long time.

"Soup lady," I called.

There was no answer, so I put on my robe and went downstairs. I found I was alone in the house, and there was no sign that anyone else had been there.

12

Freshman

———————

As I approached it, the old gray building looked cold and vacant and I began to wonder if I had the right place. But entering the hallway, I could hear Frankie Lyman and the Teenagers singing "I'm Not A Juvenile Delinquent", so I figured this must be it.

The gymnasium hardwood floor was buffed to a mirror-like finish and there were brightly colored balloons hanging everywhere.

The chubby freckle-faced girl, who was sitting by the doorway selling tickets, eyed me as I approached.

"You're not a junior, are you?" She was looking at me as though she suspected me of being underage.

"Uh no."

"Sophomore? " Her reddish eyebrows were almost touching her hairline.

"No." People were beginning to line up behind me, and my ears were getting hot.

"Well, I know you're not a senior. And if you're not a junior or a sophomore–"

"It's okay Rebecca, he's with me." John Murphy, who was a friend of my older cousin's and a senior star quarterback for Central High, said to her discreetly as he entered the gym.

"Thanks." I called to him as he walked away.

"No problem. Have fun."

So there I was, a freshman at a junior hop. I didn't know anyone and I was real shy. I was sitting on the first row of bleachers, studying the boards in the hardwood floor; "Since I Fell For You" by Lenny Welsh began to play on the hi-fi, when this female voice directly in front of me says, "Do you want to dance?"

I looked up, and standing before me was Peggy Rockwell, the most beautiful girl at Central High.

She was wearing a red velvet gown, and her reddish blonde hair was streaming down over her bare shoulders. I stood up and spun my head around, looking over both of my shoulders, then I pointed at my chest with my thumb and, trying to say me and yes at the same time, I asked, "Mess?"

She looked bewildered and then she repeated;

"It's lady's choice and I'm asking you, do you want to dance?"

I managed "Uh huh." and followed her to the dance floor.

I can still remember her fragrance as we danced. I took a deep breath and, holding her close, I whispered, "Do you like to fish?"

She looked into my eyes and began to laugh, and then she said, "You're serious?"

"Well yeah," I said, "You see, my Father owns a boat and if you like to fish, maybe we can go together sometime. I mean fishing." I was out of breath, little beads of perspiration were forming on my forehead, and my heart was beating in both my ears, like a bass drum.

She laughed hard, and then she said with a very serious demeanor, "I`ve never been fishing but it sounds like fun. Do you have to put worms on hooks and stuff?"

"Yeah, but I could show you how. It's real easy."

"How old are you?" she asked.

"Almost fifteen," I lied.

"Are you a sophomore?"

"Uh yeah." Now I was in a real jam, and I knew it.

"Do you have Miss Gladstone for English?"

"Uh huh," I said.

"What do you think of her?"

"Um, she's okay," I choked. My face was probably as red as her gown.

"Really?" she asked. "You don't think she's a little...overbearing?"

"Well yeah, I guess she is, a little."

"Is Vinny Pinto in your class?"

"Uh, yeah," I said, my confidence a shambles.

"I tricked you," she said. "Vinny graduated last year. Why are you lying? Is it because you like me?" I nodded without looking at her.

"You don't have to lie to make people who are genuine like you," she said. "Remember that."

She kissed me on the cheek when the dance

ended and smiled warmly at me as she walked away.

13

Muse

_____

Angel Ortiz watched his last five dollar chip get raked away by the pit boss at the crap table. He was only going to stop at Las Vegas for one hour, just until the next bus came through to bring him to L.A.. Here he was, two days later watching the last of his money evaporate. He started for the exit, a sick feeling in his gut and then he remembered the six quarters in his pocket. He sat at a quarter poker machine, deposited five quarters, and watched as the backs of five cards automatically flipped themselves face up as the last quarter registered.

He watched the screen while an ace of hearts, queen of hearts, nine of spades, jack of hearts, and nine of diamonds revealed themselves. He pushed the hold button on the two nines and moved his hand to the deal button.

"Wait," a woman's voice said quietly as she took the seat next to his.

"What?" he asked as he looked in her direction, surprised by her beauty.

She had long, flowing, silky black hair and almond shaped eyes that were the color of the ocean off Waikiki. Angel's eyes took in and visually digested all of her in one glance.

"Can I play your hand?" she asked. He hesitated a moment, and then even as he inhaled her fragrance and felt dizzy, he stood up and allowed her to sit at his machine. She removed the hold on the two nines and pushed the hold on the ace, queen, and jack of hearts. She had the look of an eighteen year old except for her eyes.

"Push the deal button," she said, smiling at him. He hesitated again, remembering this was the last of his money, but then he suddenly felt excited, so he pushed it. The king and ten of hearts joined the ace, queen, and jack. He watched as the machine flashed a small red light and silently began to roll digital numbers for how many quarters it would pay. It stopped at four thousand. He was still standing by the woman when an attendant arrived and counted out ten crisp one hundred dollar bills and laid them across his outstretched palm.

"Thanks," he said to the attendant who was already walking away. He turned to the woman as she stood up. "Some of this is yours," he said.

"It was your quarters," she said.?"Yeah but it was your play."?"You can buy me lunch," she said.

Angel had come to Las Vegas on his way to L.A. from Santa Rosa New Mexico with five hundred dollars to his name. He was nineteen years old, and it had taken him six months to save that much money, working on his Uncle Ramon's chicken farm.

"Let me at least give you one hundred dollars for your advice" he said. She took the hundred he held out to her as she began to walk away from him.

"Follow me," she said over her shoulder. He followed her to a twenty dollar minimum blackjack table and as she sat down, he sat uncomfortably next to her. The young lady dealer smiled professionally at them as they sat.

"Give the dealer a hundred dollars," the woman said.

"What's your name?" he asked the woman, as he handed the dealer a hundred dollars.

"Luquia," she said with a strange smile.

"Four twenty-fives," she said. The dealer placed four twenty-five dollar chips in front of him as two other people seated at the table placed their bets.

"Put up twenty-five," she said. He did and watched as a king of hearts followed his facedown card. They looked at the face down card together, and she smiled at him as they made eye-contact. "Take a hit," she said. He knew enough about blackjack to know you never hit on a seventeen, but he scratched the table with his card, and he felt a tickling sensation in his solar plexus as the dealer turned over a four. In one hour they accumulated twenty-three thousand, four hundred and eighty-seven dollars. She stood up suddenly and stretched.

"We can go now," she said. He gathered in their chips and followed her to the cashier.

"Half of this is yours," he said, holding out a roll of bills, as they left the casino.

"Put that money in your pocket before you get

rolled," she said. "What's your name anyway?" she asked.

"Angel Ortiz," he said.

"Angel? Cool name," she said, laughing, "people call me Lucky for short, and I'm going to make you one lucky angel." She stopped their walk in front of a fancy hotel and pointed at it. "Go get us the honeymoon suite," she said, winking at him and pushing him gently in the direction of the hotel.

Angel went inside and stood at the check-in counter alone, as various hotel employees rushed past him, some carrying luggage, others just looking busy and important. A smartly-dressed blonde woman in her mid-thirties came out from an office behind the counter and eyed him.

"Can I help you?" she asked without a smile. Her judgmental expression and arrogant attitude toward him were not new to Angel. He pulled the huge roll of hundred dollar bills from his pocket and laid it on the hotel counter.

"How much are your rooms?" he asked without smiling.

The woman opened a book and thumbed through it.

"How long will you be staying?" she asked.

"Two weeks," Luquia, who was suddenly standing next to him answered.

"That will be twenty-five hundred for the first week." Angel peeled off twenty-five one hundred dollar bills from the roll. The woman rang the bell for the bell boy, and Luquia and Angel followed him up to their suite.

Angel almost whistled when he saw the bedroom; it was the largest room he had ever seen, and the bed was so huge, he was sure his Mother, Father, and eight brothers and sisters could all sleep comfortably together in it. He looked at Luquia, and she pointed at the bellboy.

"Give him ten dollars," she said. Angel gave him the money without saying a word. The bellboy left, and Luquia sat on the edge of the bed. Angel looked at her, and he felt guilty.

"We made twenty-three thousand dollars," he said. "You have to take half." She looked at him briefly.

"I don't want your money," she said, "but you must follow my instructions exactly without questioning them. Do you understand?" Angel felt very strange, but he nodded and sat on the bed next to her.

"Why don't you try out the shower or bath, and I'll go after you," she said. Angel stood in the middle of the bedroom and took it all in. He walked to where the bathroom was and poked his head in before walking in. The bathroom was three large rooms. The first room was a double sink with a double mirror and lights all around them; the second room was a commode, a thing that looked like a water fountain to Angel and a shower stall; the third room had a huge circular tub with mirrors on three walls and on the ceiling. As he stood, staring at the tub, Luquia came up behind him.

"You going to have a Jacuzzi?" she asked. Angel didn't know what a Jacuzzi was, and he felt his face flush. She stepped around him, pulled the lever for the tub's plug, and began to fill the tub, while Angel silently watched. As he watched her move, Angel began to imagine how good her body would feel in his arms. He went to where she was sitting on the edge of the tub and reached out and touched her hair. She smiled without looking at him. He bent to her and tried to turn her face to him so he could kiss her, and she stood with her hands on his chest and pushed him away gently.

"You bathe and get dressed, and we'll go

downstairs and make a fortune, then, after we see what kind of a man you become, who knows?" She left the room, and Angel wondered what she meant about becoming a man. He bathed and dressed and then watched television and waited while Luquia did the same.

As they entered the hotel's casino, Angel noticed how much better everyone was dressed than they had been at the other casino. His first thought was that if they won money, he and Luquia would go clothes shopping tomorrow. He watched as she sat at the roulette wheel, and his heart beat quickly when she looked at him.

"Come sit by me," she called to him and smiled. He went to her and sat quietly by her side.

"Put twenty thousand dollars on red," she said. Angel felt himself stiffen, and he wanted to run. She was looking directly into his eyes, and he couldn't help squirming. It seemed to him everyone at the table was waiting. He swallowed hard and put the twenty thousand dollars on the table. The wheel spun, and the little ball bounced into a black spot on the wheel and rested there. Angel felt his face tighten, and his stomach began to turn. He looked at her with deep resentment and anger, and she slowly turned to him and smiled.

"Whoops," she said with a laugh. Angel said nothing. "Relax," she said as she pointed at the table. "Put the rest of your money on 5 red." He wanted to tell her to go to hell. He wanted to take her pretty, delicate neck in his hands and squeeze the life out of her right there, in front of everyone. Instead, he reached into his pocket, took the last of his money, and placed it on five red. Again the wheel spun, the little ball bounced and landed on 21 black. He looked away from the wheel and glared at her, and then he heard the dealer say:

"Winner, 5 red." He spun around and looked at the wheel, and there the little ball rested, on 5 red. He watched as a large stack of chips was placed in front of him. He started to reach for it.

"Leave it," she said.

"Are you crazy?"

"Unless that amount is all you wish, leave it," she said, "and your bet is thirteen red."

His legs felt shaky, and he was having trouble breathing, but he placed it as she had directed and won huge stacks of chips.

"Pick up your chips," she said. He took his chips

and followed her to the bar. When they were seated at the bar she looked at him. "Earlier, in the room, I told you that you must do exactly what I tell you without questioning it." Her face was intense as she spoke. "If you falter again, I'll leave—Understood?" Angel nodded. "Good," she said. "Let's go have dinner."

As they dined in the hotel's most expensive restaurant, Angel tried again to give her half of their winnings.

"I don't have any more room in my pockets!" he said. "Please take half the money." She smiled at him and held his hand, the first contact she had initiated with him.

"I can't accept any money from you, but I like gifts," she said simply.

The next morning, Angel woke up early and, while Luquia slept, he went into the bathroom and counted the money. When he was finished, he took a thousand dollars, flattened it out and put it in his shoe, then he dressed himself and went and bought them coffee and doughnuts. He gently woke her when he returned, and she sat up in bed when he handed her the coffee.

"How much money would you like to win?" she asked. Angel thought for a moment.

"One million dollars," he said.

"What will you do with a million dollars?"

"I'll buy a new house for my family, a new truck for my Uncle Ramon, a diamond necklace for you, and a Toyota Forerunner for myself. The rest I'll put in the bank." She finished her coffee and went to the bathroom. Five minutes later she returned fully dressed.

"Let's go make some money," she said.

In all his nineteen years, Angel had never met anyone like Luquia. She grew more mysterious by the minute, and he found himself loving her one moment and wanting to murder her the next.

They won fifty-six thousand dollars that day and though he always believed his heart was strong, he wasn't sure how much longer he would survive on this bumpy road to fortune.

They ordered dinner in their room that evening, and they watched a movie. After the movie, Angel filled the huge tub and called to Luquia. She came to him.

"What's up?" she asked.

"What are those holes for?" he asked, pointing at

the Jacuzzi jets. She flicked the switch controlling the water flow, and the jets spewed water. After she left, he got into the tub and let the rushing water massage his tense nerves to rest. Lying next to her in bed that night was very difficult for him. He wanted her more than he could remember wanting any woman before. Her back was to him, and he moved to her and put his lips to her neck, kissing her gently.

"No Angel," she said. "If something is to occur between us, it must not be until I say it is time. Now, go back to the bathroom and put cold water on your face and calm your desire." He reluctantly did as she told him and fell to sleep easily afterward.

The next day she made him take risks he could never make himself take on his own. He marveled at how lucky he was on every single play. He watched as the money kept accumulating and by the end of the day, the hundred dollar bills in his pockets constricted his movement.

"Let's go dancing tonight," she said in the elevator on the way up to their room. He smiled at the thought of trying to dance with all the money in his pockets.

"Sure," he said. She asked him to shower first once they were in the room and after he finished and was dressed, she called from the bathroom:

"I take a size five dress—Go buy one for me and make it bright and happy." He left her bathing and went to a women's clothing shop he had seen in the hotel mall.

"Can I help you?" a young, attractive latina-looking woman asked him as he entered.

"Yes, I'd like to buy a bright and happy size five dress for my...wife," he said. She smiled and motioned him to follow her as she walked to a rack of dresses.

"What color does she like?" she asked.

"I'm not sure, but we're going dancing tonight and I...That one!" he said suddenly, pointing at a soft golden dress with white roses embroidered on it. He was surprised at how certain he was that it would be perfect on her.

"It's gorgeous," the clerk said. "I've had my eye on it for myself, but it's too expensive for me."

He went to a jewelry shop next door and bought her a diamond necklace with matching bracelet and again was able to make his selection within moments of entering the shop. He found a men's clothing shop close by and bought himself a blue double breasted blazer, white cotton slacks, and soft leather shoes. Within forty-five minutes, Angel returned to the room, their new image under his arm.

"Perfect!" she said, as she looked at her new dress. Her face seemed to change color as she opened the smaller package and looked at the jewelry. "Thank you," she said softly, and it seemed to Angel her thank you was more profound than any recognition he had ever received in his life.

They went dancing that evening and, though Angel was an excellent dancer and people often cleared the floor and watched when he danced, this evening was Luquia's, and even Angel wanted to stop and watch her. She was the most beautiful woman he had ever seen. As they danced, he sensed something had changed between them.

Later, when the band stopped playing for the evening, and they were sitting at the table quietly, Angel reached out for her hand.

"I like dancing with you," he said. Her face changed from smiling and serene to thoughtful and a hint of troubled.

"I think, with the money you have now,

tomorrow we will reach your goal of one million dollars," she said. He smiled wryly and looked away.

"What?" she asked.

"It's just funny—Last week all it took to make me happy was a thousand dollar win; this week, a million dollars hardly means anything to me."

"You mean you want to win more than a million dollars?" she asked.

"If I say yes, will we stay together longer?"

"Angel, say what is on your mind."

"I love you," he said.

"You'll get over it—They all do," she said simply. The next morning, after breakfast, after winning his fourth pot of the day, he turned to where Luquia had been sitting, and she was not there. He waited at the same place for more than an hour before going to the cashier and cashing in his chips. He walked around the entire casino, looking at each face at each table before returning to their room. She was not there; her things were gone, and Angel was sure he would not see her again. He threw the hundred dollar bills on the bed and began to count. Including the thousand dollars he had hidden in his shoe, Angel had one million one hundred dollars, but he felt desperate to see Luquia again.

He stayed in the hotel another week and placed ads in the local newspapers and bought radio time giving descriptions of her, offering rewards of huge sums of money for her location. Finally on the last night before his departure, the phone rang.?"Hello?" a man's voice said. "Are you the gentleman looking for a woman named Luquia?"

"Yes!" Angel replied.

"Well, I know where she is, but it will cost you one million dollars," the man said.

Angel thought for a moment and then let out a long breath of air.?"Never mind," he said as he hung up.

14

Sketch

———————

As I entered the front door to the tiny corner bar, my dog Harry by my side, a hand took my elbow.

"Hey Sketch, good to see you," a woman's voice said.

"That you Katelin?" She squeezed my elbow in response.

"You want to sit in front?" she asked as she led me past the bar.

"Sure," I said, estimating from the sound of the voices that there were about forty people in the bar.

"Johnny Walker Black, straight up?" she asked as Harry and I sat down.

"And a bowl of water for Harry," I said.

Moments later I heard blues chord progressions being played on a piano. The ice in the glasses around me stopped clinking and everyone in the bar stopped talking at the sound of that first note. A woman's voice started singing the blues, and I swear, it sounded as if everyone there stopped breathing.

When the song ended and the applause began, Katelin brought my drink and Harry's bowl of water. She put my drink in my hand then she placed Harry's bowl in front of him. As I reached for my wallet, she put her face close to mine.

"Mick says your money's no good here," she almost hollered over the applause.

I always carry a sketch pad; that's why many of the folks who've seen me around the neighborhood call me Sketch. I can't comment on my work, for obvious reasons.

I drank my drink and raised my arm for another. Katelin came to my table.

"Ready for another?"

"Bring one for the singer too," I said.

Within ten minutes this girl was standing next to me. As soon as she was within three feet of me, before she said a word, I knew it was her.

"Hey, Sketch."

"You know me?" I asked.

"Seen you around the neighborhood, but I just learned your name from a guy at the bar. Thanks for the drink." I nodded.

"Mind if I sit here?"

"Please," I said coolly, but my heart was in overdrive.

She sat down next to me and I could feel her eyes on me.

"How'd you get your name?"

"Guess it's what I do," I said. There was a pause then, and I didn't want her to leave.

"Can I touch your face?" I asked. She pulled her chair very close to mine, took my hands in hers and placed them on her face. It was just as I had envisioned: the length of the forehead, the depression between the eyes, her nose, her lips, her chin, her cheekbones, her hair.

"Did you see me now?" she asked.

"Yeah, but everything is like I already knew." I said.

"What's that mean?"

"Beautiful."

"So you gonna sketch me?" she asked.

"Yeah, but I'll wait till you're up there singing," I said. We had another drink together and then she went back to the stand. Everyone stood up and applauded as she sat at the piano.

Four bars into "Stormy Monday", I took my sketch pad from my pack and began to sketch. I can't go back and fix things; when my pen goes to paper, that's it. I sketched during the whole second set and, by the end of it, I could tell there were at least three people looking over my shoulder. I closed my pad as she ended the last tune of the set and people stood and applauded while she stepped down and walked to my table.

"Did you sketch me?" she asked as she sat down. I didn't answer, I just opened the sketch pad. "You're even better than I heard," she said.

"You heard I was good?"

"I heard you were somebody who would become famous after you died," she said.

"Hmmm," I said. And then, to fill the silence, I added "Isn't the bar scene a step into hell for you?"

"Hell?"

"Yeah, I mean you're a church singer aren't you?" She laughed then and covered my free hand with hers.

"This ain't hell man, hell is four blocks west of here, right where Potomac crosses Main."

"Well," I said, "you're a slice of heaven." She laughed again.

"No, heaven is on Capital Avenue, up past Madison, where everybody's rich and white."

"So, we're somewhere in the middle?" I said.

"Yeah, it's where real people live," she said.

"Amen," I said.

After her last set, the three of us left the bar together and walked down East Avenue along the river. We stopped at a hot dog cart and she handed me a hot dog; I gave half to Harry.

"You like me cause I'm black?" she said.

"Yeah," I said. "You like me cause I'm white?"

"I'm serious, my color turn you on?"

"I can't see your color, and who says you turn me on?"

"Do I?" she asked. I thought for a moment.

"I guess it's your voice," I said.

"That enough?" she asked. I didn't know.

"What do you think?" I said.

"I think we must both be crazy for having this conversation."

"Why?" I asked.

"Because you're some blind white guy who bought a drink for a girl in a bar and you can't even look into her eyes," she said.

"Sure I can," I said, "I just can't see them, that's all." She didn't say anything for a while, and I felt uncomfortable. "You prejudiced against blind guys?" I asked.

"Naw, I ain't about to pre-judge any thing or any body," she said. "Anyway, that gives you a good excuse to be with a black woman, doesn't it?"

"What?" I said, "You think I need an excuse to be with somebody?"

"Well, you don't have to look at people's faces judging you; people cut you slack because they figure you might not even know I'm black." I felt my face burn and my eyes sting.

"Damn, that's cold," I said." What's that say about how you see yourself? There's nothing low about my standards."

"Sketch, I ain't out to hurt nobody, but this is how I see it."

"And you're blinder than I am," I said. "I can't

see you, but I heard you, I felt your face; you saw my sketch. You think other people, people who ain't blind and people who ain't black have a better understanding of each other than you and I?"

"I don't know what I think...maybe I'm a little scared," she said.

"Scared of what?" I asked. "Where's a seat? I want to sit down." She took my arm and led me to a bench where we both sat. Harry laid down by my feet with his body against my leg.

"You're the first white guy I ever liked this way and I'm having a rough time relaxing with it." I felt my shoulders relax when she said that.

"Okay," I said, "but that's what you got to tell me, not that bs about us being a couple of sorry ass misfits and that's why we're becoming friends."

"I never said that," she said. "Look, I just got off a long bumpy ride with a guy from Newark and I need a rest." I leaned back against the warm hard backrest and concentrated on the air on my face.

"Yeah girl," I said getting up, "you have yourself a rest. Home Harry." and Harry pulled me toward home.

A week went by before I thought about her again. Her face popped up like bread you forget is in the toaster. And she wouldn't go away. I couldn't understand the longing I began to feel for her company. Maybe she was right, I thought, maybe I'm a desperately lonely blind guy.

It was Saturday morning, I leashed Harry and we went out for a walk. As we passed the corner bar, I heard her voice. Harry and I stood outside until the song ended and then we continued down the block. I heard someone running behind us and getting closer.

"Sketch?" her voice said. "Is that you?"

"Hello," I said, "I don't even know your name."

"It's Veronica," she said. "I've missed you."

"Then I guess you're all rested," I said. I felt her lock her arm in mine.

"Yeah, rested" she said. "Now where were we?"

15

Translation

———————

"Ha, the truth!—You want the truth?!! Cut my heart out and you got the truth."

"Mr. Walker, I've been buyin' your records since I was eight years old, and everything I hear out of that horn sounds like the truth to me." The young journalist seated across the table from J.D. Walker, world class jazz saxophonist, stared at him with wide eyes.

Walker looked into the young man's eyes for a long time. "Bless you son, for sayin' so—but you don' know what you're talkin' about." He picked up his glass of Johnnie Walker Black and took the whole two shots plus ice in his mouth and swallowed. "How you gonna have truth when they ain't no justice?"

"Sir, aside from the social implications, could we possibly talk about the truth in art as it applies to music?"

Walker raised his arm, and a waitress brought him another drink before he spoke.

"Truth...in...art...as...it...boy, why you wanna be talkin' that gobble de gook to me? Look at me son. I'm nearly sixty years old. I been playin' the horn since I was five. I work hard, and only once in maybe a hundred gigs I touch the truth—You know why you think you hear truth in my horn? Because you don' know what truth is." The young man had been watching Walker the whole time, now he looked away. "That's right. You been buyin' eggs at the grocery store for so long that if you tasted a real egg, just come out of a chicken, you'd spit it out an' holler at the chicken."

"Mr. Walker, why do you want to deny the integrity you express on your horn sir?"

Walker downed his drink and raised his arm.

"Boy, I'm old—an' I'm tired. Why don' you find somebody else to follow with your pen an' paper?"

The young man did not move and the two of them looked into each other's faces for a long time. " Okay boy, I see you need to get your brain shook. Every time I stan' up there," he pointed at a small stage at the rear of the tiny bar, "an' do my thing, I take people away from the truth...that's right, people listen an' clap they han's an' say my, my but all I'm doin' is camouflagin' misery. I'm store-bought eggs son. I got no integrity— I'm a lazy-ass old man—You want to talk truth an' not talk about people? Don' work—No people—no possibility of truth. Us black folk, we been dancin' the soft shoe for this bullshit equal-opportunity society for so long, we barely know we're doing it anymore."

Walker finished his drink and stood up. "Interview's over; Good luck son."

The young man said nothing but, stayed seated, contemplating what Walker had said. He stayed until the club closed, and then he went home to his apartment and wrote draft after draft from his memory of what Walker told him. He fell asleep at seven a.m. and woke up at two p.m..

He showered, brushed his teeth, and read what he had written:

Honesty In Art?

I had a very interesting conversation with world-class jazz alto-saxophonist, J.D. Walker, this evening. He revealed, to me, what it is that a truly gifted and ascending artist concerns himself with. He wasted no time defining for me, the meaning of being true to one's self and the necessity of developing conscience as it relates to humanity. " Art, in it's highest form, cannot exist without a recognition of the social implications of the expression of that art." What he was saying was that art perfected, was art that expressed its dissatisfaction with humanity's lack of conscience, and that all art, in all forms, needed to express universal truths that opened the eyes of humanity. To do less, was to perpetuate and even accelerate, an already descending trend in the integrity of the expression of truth in art.

He spoke about his own playing as if it were drivel and a weak excuse to call himself an artist. He spoke about societal injustice as a plague and the need for every man, but especially the artist, to be ever aware of it, and furthermore to combat it in all its forms, inwardly and out. He spoke about the need for every artist to be extremely careful about expressing beauty without recognition of the darkness in mankind, for to do so, is to condone oblivion and apathy; the true enemies of equality. And finally, he spoke about how important it was for us to open our eyes in order to see where honesty and integrity do exist because there is so little of them, they have become almost unrecognizable.

Mr. Walker I, for one, thank you for your honesty.

16

Tony

The used red brick were as old as the old man building the sidewalk with them. They were porous and coarse and had long since, worn off any fingerprints the old man had.

He was on his knees in the sand building, and it was how he had spent most of his 75 years on planet earth. His long white hair was tied back and it made him look like an old Apache warrior.

His eyes squinted as the early-morning sun began to emerge over the hillside before him. His lean, bent body ached with the sweet pain of existence.

The old man suddenly stood and stretched his legs and back for a moment, enjoying the sensation as only a man who has used his body in that way for as long as he had could. He walked to the brick pile where he had left his thermos and poured himself a full cup. He drank deeply, savoring the taste and aroma.

He breathed in deeply, filling his lungs with the cool clean morning air and he quietly but audibly said to no one:

"All day I think about it then at night I say it; where did I come from and what am I supposed to be doing? I have no idea. My soul is from elsewhere, I'm sure of that and I intend to end up there."

He stood at the brick pile gazing at the vast open plain before him and he marveled that so much land could exist without a house or people. He thought about his Italy and about how congested and devoid of places to experience solitude it was.

He rinsed the cup with water from a trickling creek near by, put it back on the thermos, knelt back down, and resumed his work. He placed each brick carefully, using just the right amount of force with the rubber mallet to keep the surface of each brick following the terrain. Sand, brick, tap, tap, tap. He set twenty, maybe twenty-five brick, and then went back to his thermos. As he poured into his cup, he again savored the aroma and inhaled deeply, and then, as if involuntarily, his lips pronounced the words:

"This drunkenness began in some other tavern; when I get back around to that place, I'll be completely sober, meanwhile I'm like a bird from another continent sitting in this aviary. The day is coming when I fly off."

He heard an engine approaching from far off, and he shaded his eyes with his hands from the now rapidly rising sun. He stood there in this double salute as the car pulled closer and closer. And he said:

"But who's that now at my ear? Who hears my voice? Who says words with my mouth? Who looks out with my eyes? What is the soul? I cannot stop asking."

The car, a low, red sports car had by now pulled up along side of the old man.

"Tony Tony Tony. What are you doing out here?"

"I'm making a brick sidewalk."

"For who? There's nobody for miles." The man behind the wheel was middle-aged with graying temples. He was wearing a gold suit with a matching gold tie. He smiled knowingly at his companion, a blonde woman in her late twenties.

"I don't need anybody to use the sidewalk. I'm building it for myself."

"Well paisano, the sun's going to be high soon so you be careful or you'll get roasted like those brick you love so much." He drove off shaking his head.

The old man knelt again and continued his work. The sidewalk, three feet wide, and lining the highway, trimmed these wide open plains and formed a frame for even the hills beyond. He stayed on his knees for an hour this time and then hobbling back to his thermos, he quietly muttered, gazing at the sky:

"If I could taste one sip of an answer, I could break out of this prison for drunks."

He looked back at the three miles of walkway he had already built, shook his head, and almost whispered:

"I did not come here of my own accord and I cannot leave that way. Whoever brought me here will have to bring me back."

He took the cap off of the thermos and then lifted the entire thermos to his lips. The rich, red homemade wine rushed past the sides of his mouth and down his chin, over his shirt and down his pants before he tilted the thermos upright again. Wiping his mouth with the back of his hand, he hollered into the void:

"This poetry, I never know what I'm going to say; I don't plan it. When I'm outside the saying of it I get very quiet and rarely speak at all."

The italicized words are a poem entitled "Who Says Words With My Mouth" by Jelaluddin Rumi as translated by Coleman Barks.

17

Jilly

———

Early one morning, there was a knock at my door. I went and opened the door, and a boy of about twelve years old was standing there. He was a short kid with blonde disheveled hair.

His clothes were dirty, and they were much too large for him. He had a belt squeezed tight around his waist, and his pants were all bunched up at the waist. He wore a sweater and his hands weren't visible because the sleeves were so long.

"Hello," he said. "My name is David, and I live

next door. My goat, Jilly is gone, and I wondered if you saw her."

"No," I said. "How long has she been gone?"

"Well, she was home last night, but I haven't seen her all day today."

"My dog usually barks if other animals come around, so I don't think she came through here," I said.

"Would you let me know if you see her?" he asked. "I live right over there." He pointed toward the home of an old gentleman who had lived alone for as long as I lived in the area.

"You live at Mr. Kramer's place?

"Yes," he said. "He was my grandpa, but he died last Tuesday."

"Oh, I'm sorry to hear that," I said.

"Can I have a glass of milk?" he asked.

"Sorry," I said, "I don't have any milk. Would you like a glass of orange juice instead?"

"Okay." He said. I left the door slightly ajar to fetch him some juice, and he walked right in. I poured him the juice, and I stood, waiting for him to finish, and then he sat down at my kitchen table.

"This is a cool place," he said. "Are you an artist or something?"

"I try to be," I said. "and I need to get back to it, so I have to ask you to finish your juice and get back out there and look for Jilly."

My dog began to raise a fuss, so we went to the door together, and standing in my back yard was a small black goat.

"Jilly?" I asked.

"Yep," he said, and he ran outside and hugged the goat.

"Glad you found her," I called as they started walking up my driveway.

The following day, there was a knock at the door and when I opened it, the boy and the goat were standing there.

"Hello again mister, my mom says I can't keep Jilly anymore," he said. "Do you want her?" The goat looked thin and scared. She was a tiny black thing, and she made a weak goat sound. She had a rope tied around her neck, and the boy was holding the other end of the rope.

"Do I want her? No, I don't want her," I said. The kid looked like he was about to cry. "You can leave her here for now, but try to find someplace else for her." He tied the goat to a tree and left.

Four days later, he showed up at my house just as I was about to leave.

"Mister," he said, "we're moving away, and I can't take Jilly."

I had grown kind of fond of the little critter by then, so I just shrugged.

"Okay," I said. "She can stay. Good luck in your new home."

"Can I come and visit her sometimes when we're in town?" he asked.

"Sure," I said. "Where are you moving to?"

"I'm not sure," he said. "Mom said I'm going to have a new daddy and a whole new family, but I don't know where." He walked slowly up the driveway and waved to Jilly and me as he disappeared over the hill.

Jilly became a part of my little family of pets. She and Corazón, my dog became best friends, and she hardly ever left my pet pot belly pig Nigel's side. She gained weight and became deliriously happy. She did a little goat dance where ever she went, and she and Nigel roamed the entire neighborhood together daily.

Then one day, around two years later, I arrived home from town, and Jilly was gone. Nigel stood in the middle of the driveway, looking forlorn, but Jilly was gone. I looked everywhere, and I posted signs with photos I had taken of her over the years, but I received no response.

About a week later, I was at the neighborhood store and a young man stood in line in front of me. He turned slightly to face me.

"Oh hi," he said. "I've been meaning to come by and see you. I saw your signs about Jilly, and I wanted to let you know that she is fine. We've moved back to the area, and I came by and picked her up." He had grown considerably, and he appeared to be around sixteen or seventeen years old.

I was both relieved and irritated to learn of what happened to Jilly. I was glad she was alive and well. But it struck me as remarkably callous of him to not have informed me of her whereabouts.

"Thanks for finally letting me know," I said.

I heard nothing more about Jilly, and I was finally beginning to not think about her as much anymore when, while driving to the local Post Office, I saw her lifeless body along the side of the highway. I pulled over, put her into the trunk of my car and took her home to bury her.

From time to time, I would see the young fellow around. He would always greet me cheerfully, and I would always try to respond kindly, but I had trouble feeling anything but animosity toward him.

One day, while calling roll at the small community college where I teach Freshman Composition, as I was calling names and looking at their faces to put names and faces together, I read David Lanson.

"David...Lanson," I called as I looked into his face. He was smiling at me.

"Here," he said.

I have a responsibility and a commitment to remain professional at all times, and so with David I tried even harder to show no partiality one way or the other, but my disdain for him had increased. I thought of him as very irresponsible and thoughtless. As the semester progressed, he did nothing that would improve my perception of him. He missed more classes than he attended, seldom if ever turned in assignments on time, and, though cheerful, showed no real interest in academic pursuits. One day I called him aside.

"David," I said, "you have missed too many

classes, and you are not keeping up with the assigned work; you are failing this class."

"Oh, I can do better," he said. "Can you give me another chance? I'll turn in all missing work, and I won't miss any more classes."

He missed the next two class sessions, and I dropped him from my roster.

Over the ensuing years, I would see David at the local store, and he was always friendly and pleasant. He sometimes gave the impression that he was stoned. Each time I saw him seemed like a new opportunity to forgive him, and each time, I failed. My judgment and concealed dislike for him only grew.

Then one day, while looking at the poster board at the Post Office, I saw a photo of him. The text under the photo was a request for funeral donations for the young man in the photo. It was later that I learned that he had committed suicide.

I sometimes wonder if I contributed to this young man's despair. Is there something I could have done differently that would have helped him see his own self-worth?

Is it arrogance to think we have the power to change the course of events, even within our own psyches? And even if I could have turned my judgment to compassion, would it have benefitted him? Would it have benefitted me?

All I know for sure is that some part of me wants to believe I had no choice. By explaining away my responsibilities, I diminish at least some of the guilt I feel. But I suspect that even if we have no free will, we must find a way to be humane and rise above human frailties in others and in ourselves.

18

No Body

––––––––

Jessica Hall's beauty was not show stopping. The average guy could walk right past her without even noticing her. But Danny Mercer was no average guy. He saw with more than just his eyes. From the first time they made eye-contact, he saw her soul. And now, he couldn't sleep anymore; her image kept vividly appearing whenever he closed his eyes.

Jessica was twenty-five years old, and she worked in her father's office supply store. Her IQ was 142, and she read voraciously. Her colorless skin and seeming lack of humor were generally interpreted as dullness. She, in fact, had few real passions in her life, but the gathering of more knowledge was her reason for being. Danny Mercer was thirty-one years old. He had served in the military during Desert Storm and had since earned a BS in psychology. He had recently moved to the west coast from Virginia, and he knew no one in California. His loneliness did not explain, however, his obsession with Jessica. He just knew, in every fiber of his body, that if he could somehow show her who he was, she would see the undeniable compatibility of their souls and plan her life accordingly.

Jessica, for her part, seemed oblivious to his obvious interest in her. He came to the store almost every day, sometimes for staples or paperclips and sometimes for a memo pad or pen, but always to see Jessica, to hear her speak, to perhaps brush her hand with his when receiving goods or paying for them. If she smiled during the transaction, as she sometimes did, he would ponder it for hours. She noticed him, to be sure, and she was flattered by his attention, but she was not easily affected by matters of the heart. Such events were outside her domain. Falling in love is what other people did, people who sought their identity in situations that made their lives tragic, people who lived their lives as though they were operas.

"Hello," he said one morning as he approached her as she stood at the register behind the counter. "Would you like to see a movie with me this evening?" he asked, handing her a box of envelopes he wished to purchase.

She looked at him and suddenly felt compassion, and she understood at a glance, the depth of his longing. "What do you do with all this stuff you buy every day?"

He smiled broadly. "I'm thinking about opening an office supply store." She smiled, acknowledging his charm, "So?" he asked, "dinner and a movie?"

"Thank you for the offer," she said. "I'm flattered— but no." She handed him his change.

"A cup of coffee? Five minutes of your time? I don't want to be pushy, and I realize how desperate I must sound—" He looked down for a moment and was silent. It wasn't an awkward silence though. "You see, I am kind of desperate to get to know you."

She rung up and handed him his envelopes, accidentally (or was it?) grazing his hand with her own. "I'm sorry. You look like a nice guy. You shouldn't be desperate, but no thanks."?He turned crimson, but he continued to stand there, not willing to acknowledge her dismissal of him. "Look, I admit I can't stop thinking about you, but we're not seventeen. If you're not interested in romance, I would still very much like to be your friend."

She studied him for a moment, sensing his sincerity. "Why is being friends with me so important to you?"

He looked at the floor and then, slowly, gaining courage, he stood squarely and looked into her eyes. "Because life is short—I realize how Bogartian that must sound."

"How what? She asked, with just the hint of a laugh.

"Bogartian, you know, Bogart-like."

"Cute," she said with a smile. There was a long moment of silence, and then, because they made eye- contact, and she could think of nothing else to say: "You like Bogart?"

He nodded. "How about you?"

"Yes," she said, "I do." And then she said

abruptly: "Look, I have to get back to work. It's been nice talking to you though."

"Can I take that as an invitation to come in and talk with you once in a while?"

"This is a busy store," she said. "I work here and, though I think you're a nice guy, I don't have time either here or anywhere else to do much socializing."

He held up his hand in a gesture of good-bye and exited the store. Once outside, he took a deep breath and tried to decide whether to have a beer or a cup of coffee. He saw a bar a half a block away and opted for the beer.

He went into the dimly lit bar and took a seat near the opened front door.

"I'll have a tall Bud Draft," he called to the vague outline approaching him from the other side of the bar. Three beers later, he realized how good the beer tasted. Six beers later, he became cognizant of how emotionally ruffled he had become because of his encounter with Jessica.

By the eighth beer, any sense he had flew to the wind. He started ordering straight shots of tequila. He was not normally a drinker, and two and a half hours, twelve beers, and six shots of tequila later,

Jessica came into the bar. Danny's head was slumped over, and he would occasionally mutter profanities to himself. He didn't see her as she quietly took the stool next to his.

After fifteen minutes and a vodka Collins (the only drink she knew by name) she was sure he was too far gone to notice her, and she stood up to leave.

"Jessica? Is that you?" he asked, finally noticing her. He suddenly seemed sober.

"Are you alright?" she asked.

"That depends on what you mean by alright," he said. "Are you really here, and if so, why?"

"Is that a trick question?" she asked, "and if so, what must I pay if I give the wrong answer?"

"Maybe there is no wrong answer. Maybe your payment is also your reward." All during their little exchange, they kept an intense eye-contact. "So—?"

"I was on my way home when I saw you through the opened doorway...I...wanted to be sure you were okay."

"And are you sure now?" he asked.

"Yes," she said, getting up to leave, "you seem okay, good-bye."

"Wait," he said. "I'm not okay. I need your help," he called after her as she left the bar.

On the way home, she kept replaying the episode and wondered how she could have been so stupid. The one drink she had, made a huge impact on her mental and emotional state, and that plus her limited experience in dealing with men, made the events of the evening larger in her mind than they actually were. She vowed to herself that any further exchanges with him would be about office supplies only.

The moment Jessica walked out of the bar, Danny fell back into his stupor. He stayed until the bar closed and kept muttering about what a strange creation women were.

The next morning he felt a chill and reached for covers, but there were none. His entire body ached, and slowly he realized he was lying on pavement. 'Behind every lousy drunk' he thought. When he was able to focus, he noticed he was lying in a doorway. He reached up for the door handle to help him stand and when he was half way up, the store's alarm went off.

He stood on legs that felt foreign to him and try as he may, he couldn't get them to move. Moments later, as he stood in front of the store, the police arrived.

"They're going to lock my ass up," he muttered to himself.

Later, after the police read him his rights, they handcuffed him and put him in the back seat of the squad car. From the back seat of the squad car, he looked at the doorway where he had spent the night, and for the first time, he realized it was the entrance to Hall's Office Supplies. He wondered how he could ever convince Jessica that he was a worthwhile guy when he constantly acted like a fool.

At 7:30 A.M. Jessica's alarm clock and phone rang simultaneously.

"Hello?...Yes, we own Hall's Office Supplies...A burglar?...I'll be right there." She brushed her teeth, got dressed, and drove to the store. When she pulled up, Danny was still sitting in the squad car. She looked at him and he looked away.

She exited her car and walked over to the group of police officers who were by then drinking coffee and laughing.

"Good morning," she said. "I'm Jessica Hall, the owner of the store's daughter. The man you have in custody is a regular customer at our store. He may have set off the burglar alarm but he is not a burglar."

The lead officer stepped toward her. "Are you sure ma'm?"?She nodded.?"May I see some ID please?"

She gave him her driver's license and after looking at it and writing her name in a pad, he gave her a piece of paper to sign, after which they released Danny.

When the police left, she looked at him, shook her head and without saying a word, went and opened the store. Danny, humiliated beyond reason, stumbled down the street toward his apartment. The route he took to his apartment took him past the bar of the previous evening and as he approached it, he felt nauseous. He fell to all fours and vomited for quite awhile. "Fitting," he said aloud as he stood up. He felt slightly better.

He walked the rest of the way to his apartment and went directly to bed.

At 2:30 that afternoon, while dreaming about Jessica, his ringing phone woke him up. "Hello?" he answered on the third ring. There was a pause.

"Welcome to the land of the living," came

Jessica's voice. "Is that what you call this?" He smiled into the phone.

"Well, most people I know do, yes." She noticed her hand was shaking, her heart was beating harder than usual, and there was something wrong with her voice. This recognition bothered her so much, she almost hung up the phone.

"I was just dreaming about you." He felt a shot of adrenaline pump through his pickled brain, and he marveled at the contrast.

"Oh? You weren't out of line, were you?" she asked. She played back her words before he spoke, and she wished she could unsay it.

"Ended too soon, but in my dream you told me you liked me a lot."

"Gotta go, a customer just came in," she said. Would you like to meet me for coffee this evening at 6 at Tony's Deli?"

"I'll be there..."he said. There was a click at the other end. He turned on the television, laid on the bed, and fell asleep. He woke up at 5 and began to wonder if she really had called or if he had only dreamt it.

At 5:45 he took a back corner table at Tony's deli, and tried to calm down. When 6 o'clock arrived and Jessica had not, he began to doubt everything. By 6:05 he was sure his mind had played a trick on him. Always punctual himself, it didn't occur to him that a given time to some people meant roughly. At 6:15, he stood up to leave.

"Going so soon? Jessica said behind him as he was unhooking his jacket from the back of his chair.

"I believed I had dreamt the whole thing."

"Who's to say? Maybe you still are," she said.

"Well do me a favor, if this is a dream, put out the 'Do Not Disturb' sign ".?As they sat down, he marveled at how beautiful she looked and at how her beauty seemed to increase each time he saw her.

"Are you a figment of my imagination?" he asked

"Unfortunately, yes, I am... And I imagine you also. Eventually though, if you and I become friends and hang out together, we won't imagine each other quite so much." They ordered cappuccinos.

They talked and drank coffee late into the night, and one of the workers began to mop the floors. Neither of them wanted to call it a night, so, once outside, they walked awhile. When the bar crowd started leaving the bars, Danny and Jessica went to Danny's apartment.

As Danny put the key into the lock of the door to his apartment, Jessica touched his hand that held the key. "Danny, I'm only here to continue our conversation, okay?" Her face was furrowed with lines of worry. "Let's not ruin things," she added.

Without opening the door, he took his hand off of the key and held her hand.

"I'm honored and grateful that you trusted me enough to come here," he said. "The last thing in the world I would wish to do is to ruin things."

She smiled, comforted by the tenderness in his voice as well as the words that he spoke. He opened the door, turned on a soft light in the living room, motioned her to the sofa, put a cd of Laurindo Almeida on the sound system, and brought two glasses of Chablis in what seemed to be one motion.

When he came into the room with the Chablis, she was, from her seated position, taking in the room.

"Do you like it?" he asked.

"Very much," she said. "It seems so much like what I know of you."

The room, like the rest of the apartment, was modest, but what little decor there was, had been intentionally selected for harmony of color and to the details of what appealed to him. All indications, from what was visible, were that this was a man who knew himself. Danny Mercer was indeed a modest man, a modest man with impeccable taste in all things. He owned few possessions, but what he owned was of the highest quality. His relationships with people were formed in much the same way; he selected his closest friends, the friends in whom he was willing to invest time and energy, by the highest standards. If, however, he was hard on others, he was twice as hard on himself.

Jessica leaned back in the sofa and closed her eyes, holding her wine glass on her tummy with both hands. She hadn't lied; she loved this room, and it truly did seem like a reflection of this man. The wine allowed her to have such thoughts without the usual panic that accompanied them. She opened her eyes, and for the first time, she began to look at each item in the room. Her first impression hadn't been an intellectual one; her first impression had been more like a fragrance than something visual. She looked down at the floor and noted a wonderfully simple blue Persian rug. It had a tan border, and it was surrounded by highly polished hardwood flooring. In the corner stood a low oak table with a red thick glass vase on it. In the vase were four fresh red roses. The walls were painted a very light color with just a hint of gold tint. On the wall, behind where she sat, hung a huge print of The Polish Rider by Rembrandt. On the wall to her right, stood a large bookcase filled to capacity with books that were mostly about psychology and philosophy. She stood up and walked over to the bookcase.

"You read a lot?" she asked, pulling Meditations of Marcus Aurelius from one of the shelves.

"Occasionally," he said, as he came and stood by her while she read.

"Never allow yourself," she began to read aloud and then he joined in without looking at the book, "to be swept off your feet: when an impulse stirs, see first that it will meet the claims of justice; when an impression forms, assure yourself first of its certainty."?They stood very close and laughed together. Both became serious in the same instant, and they kissed. It was a long, sensual, gentle kiss, and it was filled with promise for both of them.

"I better be going," she said, putting the book back in its place.

"Okay. I'll walk you home," he said as he turned off the sound system.

There was a crescent moon hanging low in the sky. It was 3:30 am, and they were both tired. As they crossed a four-way intersection, a car came speeding full bore at the light. They were in the cross walk, crossing with the green light and the driver never saw them. Danny saw what was about to occur, and he pushed her with such force that she landed almost on the opposite curb. He took the left front fender of the speeding car on his right hip, and the impact threw him thirty feet into the air. He came down with a hollow thud; the car continued with its same speed, and Jessica stood up and ran to where Danny lay. He was bleeding from his mouth, nose, and eyes, and blood was seeping through his clothing from various other locations. She lifted his hand in hers. He opened his eyes.

"Are you okay?" he asked. She smiled, and then

she heard him exhale one long breath as his body went limp.

Jessica didn't cry. There was a dry, hard coating to her feelings that neither crying nor words nor even thoughts could penetrate. She was, of necessity, emotionally shut down.

One week later, she attended Danny's funeral. She stood to the rear of the small gathering and left before the services were over. She drove directly to Danny's apartment, found the manager, and leased it for one year. She went up to the apartment, let herself in, and sat on the sofa she had sat in the last evening they were together. She looked at the red vase, which now held dry, dead roses: no color, no fragrance, no life.

And then she felt a presence. Nothing visible, but something or someone was beside her on the sofa. She closed her eyes, and she was sure she felt lips brush her cheek. She wasn't frightened. She didn't want to move. She wanted only for the presence to stay—forever. She felt a soft pressure, like a hand caressing her hair, and she felt rather than heard non-verbal whispers of love in her ears. She swooned for a moment, and then she stood up, walked to the bedroom, took off her clothes, and lay on the bed. She immediately felt him next to her. He caressed her body with his hands and his lips until she glowed and then he made love to her. She felt this lovemaking had somehow freed her soul.

She woke up in his bed the next morning. She looked to her right and left on the bed and saw nothing. And then she felt arms encircle her and fingers caress her temples. She felt ecstasy as lips brushed her ear and kissed the nape of her neck. She opened her eyes and tried to see him, but she could see nothing. She reached out to where she was sure he would have to be, but there was nothing tangible there. All indications were that she had imagined all of it, and then the fingers gently caressed her face. And she let go of looking for visible signs and gave herself instead, to the sensations that his mere touch produced.

Later that morning, Jessica dressed herself and went to work. As customers came into the store and made their purchases, she put the items in bags, gave them receipts, and gave them their appropriate change, but all her actions were done without her; she was on automatic pilot. She tried once or twice to be more present to what she was doing, but somehow, her soul seemed to have vacated the premises.

After work that evening, since there was still an hour's worth of daylight, she decided to go for a walk in a small park near the store. In the center of the park was a lake with an island that was connected to the shoreline by a small footbridge. She walked to the center of the bridge and stood, gazing at the water, contemplating the events of the previous evening. 'Did what seem to happen really happen? Could there be some kind of carry-over whereby a spirit can exist on this plane without a body?' She knew from her own experiences that many bodies existed without spirits, but that was different- – bodies without spirit were somehow more understandable. 'Under what conditions could life (if life could) exist without a body? Or does life of the body constitute life? If there is life after death, meaning life of the body, are there restrictions on where that life can exist? And if life can exist here without a body, are there many lives existing now, in our presence?'

A young couple passing the bridge stared at her for a moment and then moved on. She noticed them and realized that she had been speaking aloud and that her volume had been steadily increasing. She decided to go to Danny's apartment and, if his spirit was there, to ask him all of these questions.

After entering the apartment, she poured two glasses of Chablis, put Laurindo Almeida on the cd player, and sat on the sofa. She waited patiently, but nothing happened.

"Danny," she said quietly, but out loud. "Are you here? I need to talk to you." There was no response, neither that evening, nor any evening in the ensuing weeks that followed. It was as if her evening of lovemaking with Danny's spirit never happened—until one morning, she woke up extremely nauseated and made it to the bathroom just in time to throw up. She felt ill, and she was puzzled until she remembered that she had also missed her menstrual cycle that month. She had not been sexually active in over a year prior to her experiences with Danny's spirit, which she was not even sure had happened anymore.

She stood up, brushed her teeth, got dressed, and called for an appointment with her doctor. That afternoon, she learned she was, indeed, pregnant. Jessica continued to work, and the weeks and months passed quickly as she grew bigger and bigger. On the morning she went into labor and was rushed to the hospital, she began to worry. 'What if it's a monster?' She began to wish that she had terminated its development. And then, suddenly it was in her arms. All of her fears faded as she cuddled the baby boy, Daniel. Others in the room hid their eyes from hers and shook their heads solemnly as she embraced the empty blanket.

19

Lulu

___

Lulu Montez ate a bowl of ice cream every morning. She said it was because she was so hot. She was twenty-four years old when I met her. We started living together on her twenty-fifth birthday. She said I was her birthday gift to herself. I threw a big birthday party for her at our place. There must have been sixty people packed into our tiny apartment. That was two months ago, and people still talk about how good the cake was. I hired a friend of mine to make it, and he put a whole quart of rum in it. Nino Fuego brought his guitar and a friend of his who played bongos. People were dancing everywhere, even out in the hallway. At one point Lulu started singing La Bamba, and the whole crowd started singing with her.

She and I met during a ceramics class we were taking at State. I was making this Buddha statue, and she came over to me to check it out.

"That's pretty cool," she said. "Are you a Buddhist?"

"Naw," I said. "I just like the shape."

"How about me?" she said. "Do you like my shape?" She went and stood a few feet away and assumed a model pose.

"Yeah, you're cool," I said. "Can you say wise things in Chinese?"

"If I say yes, will you make a statue of me?"

"Only if you prove it," I said. She started rattling off gibberish words that probably sounded Chinese to her. We laughed.

"So, are you going to ask me out?" she said.

"I don't know; what's your name?" I said.

"Lulu"

"Lulu? Naw, I don't go out with Lulus."

"Okay then, my name is Delores," she said.

"How's Friday night?" I said.

"I'll have to check my calendar," she said. And then she walked away. She was really cute. Short, thin, but shapely, and she had the most amazing green eyes!

On the way out of class that day, this tall skinny guy walks up to me and hands me a folded slip of paper. I unfolded it, and it read 427 6093 – Delores

I called her after school that day.

"Delores?" I said

"No, this is Lulu," she said. "You must have the wrong number."

"How's Friday night?" I asked.

"Okay, but what's your name?"

"Sam"

"Sam," she said. "Yeah, I like it. You look like a Sam."

She told me where she lived, and I picked her up at seven Friday night. She was even cuter than I remembered. We went to this little dive bar named Jocko's, where they serve burgers and mixed drinks.

When our food arrived, we ordered a second round of drinks. I was having fun, and I was thinking about what kind of movie she'd like after dinner.

"You like me?" she said.

"You're okay," I said.

"Just okay? You don't think I'm fabulous?"

"You're a little fabulous," I said.

"Just wait till you get to know me," she said. "You'll think I'm adorable."

So, a couple of months later, on her birthday, she moved in.

The morning after she moved in, she was sitting on the bed eating her ice cream when I woke up. She looked at me as I opened my eyes.

"Human cranial receptors were not intended to be ignored," she said.

"Huh?" I said, " What're you talking about?"

"We see; we hear; we smell; we taste," she said, "but at least half the population of America does not think."

I sat up in bed. "What are you going on about? Does not think about what?" I said.

"Think about anything," she said. "Our country is on a path to self-destruction because so many people are on automatic pilot."

"Lulu,," I said, "it's nine o'clock in the morning. Are you sleep talking?"

"No," she said, "I just heard a TV news guy say that a crazy man has been elected our next president."

"Oh?" I said. "How do you know he's crazy?"

"See?" she said. "That's exactly what I'm talking about. We're all asleep at the wheel."

"What wheel?" I asked as I stood up and stretched.

"Our cranial receptors are not engaging with our brains," she said. "We see; we hear, but we're not processing the information that would help us make intelligent decisions."

"Oh?" I said, "What intelligent decisions would you like us to make?"

"Right," she said. "That's just the point; what can be done?"

"Did you make coffee yet?" I asked her.

"Yeah, it's on the stove," she said.

I went and poured myself a cup. She was still in the bedroom.

"You want a cup?" I called to her.

"Okay," she said. "I think we should move."

"Move?," I said, "move where?"

"I don't know, Mexico or somewhere, " she said. "Maybe we can help them build that wall."

"What wall?" I asked. "The wall is in China. And it's been built for a long time."

"Oh God," she said as I entered the bedroom with her coffee. "Are you that clueless?"

"You're welcome," I said, handing her the coffee.

"Don't you see what's happening?" she asked. She really was adorable.

"Yes," I said, "I see what's happening; you're losing your marbles."

"Sam," she tugged at my arm. "We've got to get the hell out of here."

"Get out of here," I said. "But Lulu, you just got here."

"Please don't make jokes," she said.

"Okay," I said, "first rule of going somewhere is having a destination in mind."

"Okay ,"she said. "I've thought about it. Let's go buy airline tickets to New Zealand."

"New Zealand!? Why New Zealand?"

"I hear it's beautiful there," she said. " We can go fishing every day and live on what we catch, and pineapples."

"And this is what happened when you thought about it?" I asked.

She was smiling by now.

"Uh huh," she said. "And they even speak English there, so we wouldn't have to learn a new language."

"Well, I got to get to class," I said as I kissed her and headed for the door.

"Will you at least think about it?" she called to me as I left.

In the two weeks that followed, her demeanor had changed; she had become quieter and more subdued. She wasn't even having her morning bowl of ice cream.

"No ice cream this morning?" I asked one morning.

"I forgot to buy some," she said.

"But how can you cool your hotness without ice cream?" I said, thinking she'd at least smile, but she didn't.

"Should I go to the store and buy you some?" I asked.

She shook her head no. I went to her and kissed her on her forehead.

Then one day, when I came home from class, she was gone.

I found a note on the kitchen table.

Sam, My Love,

I can't stay here anymore. I'll always love you, and I hope with all of my heart that you find life unbearable without me and decide to follow me half way around the world. I'll write to you when I'm settled in my new home.

Love Always,

Lulu

P.S. There's a pint of butter pecan in the freezer for you. Sorry, gotta go.

And like that, she was gone. That was a week ago, and now I'm sitting here at my desk in class, wondering what the hell happened. Hurricane Lulu struck and left a path of destruction where Sam used to be. I can't sleep; I drink most of my meals; I have trouble talking to people, and I'm still waiting for Lulu to send me her new address.

20

The Making of a Mad Man

_____

♥

I was ten years old the first time I saw her. I was playing with Donna, Reverend Williams' daughter; we were in the front yard playing tag. After hours of hearing blues chord progressions being played on a piano from somewhere within the house, some movement caught my attention from above where we stood. As I looked up at the third floor stoop, a striking young woman leaned over the railing. She had huge naked white breasts, long red hair, and eyes that flashed blue even from where I stood, gazing at her.

She looked down at me as I stared up at her. Donna looked up to see what I was staring at.

"That be crazy ole Miss Rose," she said.

"How'd she get here?" I heard myself ask.

"She from New Jersey or someplace like dat," Donna said. "She crazy like a frog, daddy said, but she play piano good, and she know the gospel too."

The next time my momma visited, I told her about Miss Rose.

"Momma," I said, as she pulled the old Studebaker into the driveway, "I saw a beautiful girl who played piano across at Reverend Williams' House." Momma frowned at me, and then, as she got out of the car, she hit me in the back of the head with her open hand.

"I told you to stay away from them niggers," she growled.

♥

I was in Paci's market the next time I saw Miss Rose. I was cashing in some empty pop bottles for some change to go have an eggplant grinder at Barlletto's Tavern, and she was standing in line behind me. Her perfume filled the tiny store and made me feel dizzy.

Connie Ruggerio gave me fifty cents for the bottles.

"I brought thirty bottles," I said; "that's sixty cents." Connie laughed at me.

"You only brought twenty-five," she said. I felt my face burn.

"Call it," Miss Rose shouted at Connie as she flipped a quarter in the air and caught it on the back of her hand."

"Heads," Connie shouted.

"If you're right," Miss Rose said, "you get the quarter. But if you're wrong, you give this young fella his dime." Connie nodded and Miss Rose uncovered the quarter.

Connie's face was real red as she handed me my dime.

♥

I was hiding under Reverend Williams' porch the next time I saw Miss Rose. I was waiting there to scare Donna when she came outside, but before she could, Miss Rose came out and sat on the porch with a scruffy, overweight white guy. He was breathing heavy.

"I love you, Rosie," he grunted. I could see them through the cracks between the floorboards of the porch.

"Benny," she said, "you eat; you shit; you sleep. That's all you do." Benny's mouth hung open as she disappeared from the cracks in the floor, and I heard the door to the house close gently.

♥

When I heard the screams, I ran down the steps of my stoop, down to the end of my street where it met the railroad tracks, and I stood watching as others gathered. The police and ambulance came screeching to the scene, sirens blasting. The police began to cordon off the entire area with saw horses and yellow tape. One bloody limb protruded from the rail nearest me. It stood vertically with a piece of clothing attached to it. It looked like a flag of some sort as a breeze caught the fabric and flapped it. I couldn't tell whether the limb was an arm or a leg.

As I stood watching from my side of the tracks, I saw Billy Catchings, a schoolmate of mine, on the other side of the tracks and, at the same moment, I felt a hand on my shoulder. I felt an almost painful sensation as my attention was divided in two as the hand on my shoulder squeezed and Billy fell to his knees. Even as I watched his body shake with sobs, I turned to see the owner of the hand, and though it had only been a month since I had last seen her, I did not immediately recognize Miss Rose.

"I think you've seen enough," she said. "Come with me, and don't look back."

As it dawned on me who she was, I took her outstretched hand and walked with her.

She listened as I told her about my schoolmate Billy Catchings and about his momma's limb that stood like a flag. She held me as I shook and then she pushed me away from her, and at arms length, she studied my face.

She took my face in both of her hands and kissed me in the center of my forehead and then she walked away.

♥

I didn't see Miss Rose again for about five years.

He threw a round house and I caught it on my forearm. He tried to kick me with his engineer boots and I sidestepped, grabbed his heel while his foot was in the air, and he landed on his back.

"I don't want to fight you," I said.

"Fuck you," he snarled as he got to his feet. He

came at me again, and I slipped his punch and landed a right cross with my entire hundred and fifteen pounds. His nose bled profusely, and while he rolled on the ground holding his face, I walked slowly past the gathering group of onlookers and sat on a bus stop bench. When a bus arrived, I got on without looking at the number. I was shaking, and my right wrist ached from the punch I had landed. I rubbed my wrist as I looked out the window, and I felt someone sit next to me.

I turned to see the person, and Miss Rose half glanced at me as she read a newspaper. She didn't seem to notice me as I stared at her. I wanted to say something to her, but I was afraid I would sound stupid.

We sat quietly, side by side, her reading her paper and me hardly able to stop myself from screaming her name and telling her I was crazy in love with her. When she stood after a few stops and buzzed the driver, I stood too and followed her off the bus.

"Do I know you?" she asked me over her shoulder as the bus pulled away from the curb.

"Uh, I don't think so," I stammered, "but I know you—You're Miss Rose." She laughed and put her hand in the crook of my elbow as we walked side by side. We walked to the doorway of a tiny pub, and she brushed my lips with hers.

"Good-bye Kiddo," she said. "Don't let the world turn you into a zombie."

She disappeared behind the door, and I watched through the huge plate-glass window as she sat at a piano and started to play the blues.

I listened to the entire first set as a very light mist fell. Later, in my room, I cried.

About the Author

After receiving an advanced degree in Creative Writing, Samuel Provenzano began a career as a writer and instructor of composition at a community college in Northern California where he currently resides with his beautiful wife.

"I owe all my good fortune to the great Kharma that was passed on to me by those who came before," he said, smiling.

"I hope my stories add something meaningful to your life."

CPSIA information can be obtained
at www.ICGtesting.com
Printed in the USA
FSOW01n1556070118
43115FS

9 780998 574936